Peter Becomes a Trail Man

Peter Becomes a Trail Man

THE STORY OF A BOY'S JOURNEY
ON THE SANTA FE TRAIL

ORIGINAL STORY BY

William G. B. Carson

REVISED BY

William C. Carson

ILLUSTRATIONS BY

Pat Oliphant

UNIVERSITY OF NEW MEXICO PRESS

ALBUQUERQUE

Dedications

1965
Peter Carson
his book

2002
Peter's sisters
Katie, Amy, and the memory of Meggie
and his cousins Chapin and Laura
and the next generation
Elizabeth, William, Molly, Grant, Audrey, and Deirdre

LIBRARY OF CONGRESS CATALOGING-IN-PUBLICATION DATA

Carson, William G. B. (William Glasgow Bruce), 1891–
Peter becomes a trail man : the story of a boy's journey
on the Santa Fe Trail / original story by William G. B. Carson ;
revised by William C. Carson ; art by Pat Oliphant.—1st ed.
p.   cm.
Summary: In the 1850s, twelve-year-old Peter takes his dog and heads west on the Santa Fe
Trail to find his father, guided by "Uncle" Seth, who leads their wagon train through
an Indian attack, desertion by greenhorns, a buffalo stampede, and other hardships.
ISBN 0-8263-2895-4 (cloth : alk. paper)
1. Santa Fe National Historic Trail—Juvenile fiction. [1. Santa Fe National
Historic Trail—Fiction. 2. Frontier and pioneer life—West (U.S.)—Fiction.
3. Dogs—Fiction. 4. Indians of North America—Fiction. 5. West (U.S.)—Fiction.]
I. Carson, William C., 1928– II. Oliphant, Pat, 1935– ill. III. Title.
PZ7.C24245 Pe 2002
[Fic]—dc21
2002003995

DESIGN: Mina Yamashita

Contents

1

Peter Starts a Fight

"Look out there! Jump!"

The loud, harsh voice came from almost over Peter's head. He did not stop to see what was threatening him as he watched a steamboat being loaded, but leaped to the ground from his perch on top of a bale of hemp. He was just in time. A huge wagon topped by a series of large hoops clattered over the stones. It was pulled by a pair of large black mules being lashed by a burly man with a long beard. The wagon banged and swayed as it passed, one wheel striking the bale on top of the pile where Peter's leg had been a second before. It careened down the levee to the water's edge, scattering men and beasts as it went. Men shouted and cursed as they leaped to safety, but could not drown out the hearty voice of the driver—"Hey-yey-hey!"

One look was enough for Peter. He made sure that his companion, a small light brown dog, had also escaped injury and then raced after the wagon down to the river. Dozens of great steamboats with their bows shoved hard against the limestone shore were lined up along the levee. Their tall black stacks resembled a row of charred and branchless trees. The ships varied in size, but most rose to the towering height of three decks, massive structures of carved wood with many thin, spindly columns supporting the decks above them. Because the strong current of the Mississippi had carried the sterns downstream, each ship touched the shore at a slant. The gangplanks had been lowered, so that the black roustabouts could carry freight aboard.

The bearded man pulled his mules to such a sudden a stop near one of these ships that they were almost thrown back on their haunches. By the time the boy and the dog had caught up, the driver had leaped from the back of the left mule and was roaring at an officer who blocked the end of the plank resting on the levee. He had yelled, "Can't go aboard!"

"And why not? I've paid my fare an' the boat han't gone."

"You're too late," answered the officer in a surly tone. "We're pulling out in five minutes."

"Five minutes, mon!" cried the driver in a Scotch burr that became broader as he became angrier. "That's time enough to catch up a whole train, let alone one wagon! Here's my paper," and he waved a bill beneath the officer's nose. "I've paid my good silver—no mon can keep me off. If you don't call some o' your fellows here to pull me on, I'll drive on, mules an' all. An' not wan copper cent wull I pay for the baists!" he added with a prolonged rr at the end of the copper. "Which wull ye have? Make up yer mind. Ye've only four minutes noo."

"There's no room left." But the officer was weakening.

"Then find some. Ye can put me in the snag-chamber if there's no place else, an' take ten dollars off the fare. Here you, Eb, unhitch these critters," he called to a black boy who was crouched in the body of the wagon.

The officer surrendered and ordered some of the roustabouts to haul the wagon on board and clear a place for it on the first deck. Meanwhile the Scotsman stood back, hands on hips, to oversee the job.

"Please, sir, are you going to Santa Fe or Oregon?"

The big man turned and found himself staring down into the blue eyes of a small boy of about twelve whose dominant characteristics were a pug nose and a badly mussed crop of tow hair. The boy wore a pair of faded blue trousers held insecurely in place by one ancient suspender that seemed about to come apart under the strain. His bare feet were, if possible, grayer than the shirt under the suspender.

The man peered at him keenly. "And how do ye know I'm going to one or the other?" His eyes were sharp, but his voice was not unkind.

"I know by your wagon, sir."

"Santa Fe, lad. Santa Fe if the good Lord spares my old hide that long. It's a long way and a hard one. You aren't wantin' to go yerself?"

Chapter One

The boy nodded. "My Pa's there."

"Mebbe I know yer pa. What's his name noo?"

"Abel Blair, sir."

"Abel Blair . . ." the man began. "To be—hey there, take care how you handle them mules. I don't want my brains knocked out by them before giving the Injuns a chance! Take 'em back to your master. I've paid for the hire of 'em. An' watch out they don't kill any folk on the way. I'll get myself some good ones when I reach Independence."

He turned to watch the black boys pull his wagon up the gangplank. "Easy there! That's a noo cart, an' it's got a long trip ahead of it. If any one of you breaks a part of it, I'll break his head. Be sure o' thot."

In a moment he remembered the waiting boy and turned back to him. "So you're Abel Blair's lad. Your name Abel too?"

"No sir—Peter. He left me here in St. Louis while he . . ."

A bell on the top deck began to ring, and the roustabouts seized the rope and jerked it to pull the gangplank in. The big man had to jump to get aboard.

"Well, Peter, if I see yer pa, I'll tell 'im I saw you. Anythin' special you want me to tell 'im?" He had to shout above the din.

"Yes, sir." Peter called back. "Please tell 'im . . ."

There was a loud blast from the whistle and the great side-wheels began to turn under their hoods, churning the muddy water into yellow froth. The boy's reply was lost in the noise. His eyes grew bigger and bigger as he watched the tall packet back slowly from the shore with a great churning of water, screeching of ropes, and clanging of the brass bell. The bearded traveler stood on a lower deck beside his new wagon. He waved a great brown hand and tried in vain to catch the words Peter was frantically shouting. Peter ran down to the water's edge, so close that the yellow waves raised by the side wheels washed over his bare feet. He tore off his battered hat and waved it over his head, as the Prairie Princess squared about in the river, which pushed her downstream before she overcame the current and turned her nose upstream with great puffs of smoke belching from her stacks.

The little dog, evidently feeling that something was expected of him, answered the boat's whistle with a mournful howl. But his owner did not hear him. He stood motionless until the steamboat was hidden from sight by the others tied to the bank and had disappeared up the mighty, mysterious river.

As he stood watching the smoke blow across the blue sky, the boy's lip trembled. He turned suddenly, edged his way among the barrels of lard and sacks of potatoes, and then made his way up the levee toward the ugly shops and warehouses that formed the river front of St. Louis in the early 1850s.

He was followed by the faithful little dog whose compact body seemed to include the strains of every breed of canine that had ever explored the narrow streets or hunted rats in the alleys of the bustling city. The shape of his head was unmistakable evidence of some, perhaps distant, poodle ancestry. The triangular little face featured a coal-black nose and a perky tuft of hair, which was white when clean. He ran behind his master, as usual holding up his left hind leg.

The pair reached Front Street in a minute and left the Mississippi behind them. They turned up Walnut Street, which seemed like a narrow tunnel because of the buildings on its edge. The dog, obviously feeling more at home and independent, darted ahead.

A red-haired boy, somewhat larger and heavier than Peter, came out of a doorway on the left and stumbled over the dog. He screamed, "Get out, you yellow cur!" and aimed a kick at his ribs. Either his aim was not good or his intended victim was too quick, for he missed and almost lost his balance.

The older boy's offence was not very serious, but Peter needed some outlet for his emotions and did not stop to consider the justice of his cause or the possible cost of his actions. He was at the other boy in an instant and punched him in the jaw as hard as he could. It was so unexpected that it knocked the boy back against the wall of the house. It did not take him long, however, to regain his footing and fight back.

Peter put his head down and was at him again, landing blows with more spirit than effect. But this time his opponent was ready. Moreover, he was bigger and stronger. He planted a blow on Peter's upturned nose and then another on his temple. The nose spurted blood. The ancient hat came down over both eyes. But Peter was not one to know when he was beaten. He seized the bigger boy by the shirt, pulling the tail out in

He screamed, "Get out, you yellow cur!"
and aimed a kick at his ribs.

Peter Starts a Fight

the process. The stranger now caught him by his one suspender, and the struggle was on in earnest. They clinched. They tugged. They pulled. And, whenever they could, got in a punch. Crash! Down they went onto the cobblestones. The cause of it all barked hysterically and tried to find an opening to help his champion, but the two boys rolled over and over so quickly that even Brownie could not tell who was who.

Of course, all the hubbub attracted an audience. Passersby stopped and people ran out of nearby houses, the men shouting encouragement while the women protested in vain. The wildly excited little dog leaped about the two combatants, barking furiously.

"Here! Here! What's going on?" A stout little red-faced man in the black habit of a Catholic priest stopped on the narrow sidewalk.

"Looks like a fight, yer rev'rence," replied one of the onlookers, a slightly embarrassed workman in overalls.

"Now raly, is it?" asked the priest in mock surprise. "I didn't mistake it for a council of peace. Well—" he peered at the fighters over his glasses. Peter was now on the bottom. "A fight's a good thing now and then, but this wan has gone on long enough, and the little chap's got no fair chance." He bent over the two. "Here you, stop it! Do you hear me? Stop this at once!"

The boys would not have obeyed the command even if they had heard it over the barking.

So the priest caught them with two hands that were surprisingly strong. "Shut up, you little baist! No wonder they can't hear!" He pulled the larger boy off his opponent. "Shame on ye, Bill Blake, strikin' a little shaver like that!"

"I didn't start it, Father," protested Bill, rubbing a rapidly swelling eye. "He hit me first!"

Peter scrambled to his feet. "You kicked my dog!" And he advanced on him again.

"Hold on! We've had enough war for today. Bill, you go along about your business, if you have any, which I doubt. Lave this one to me."

Somewhat sullenly Bill walked off, not daring to dispute matters with the clergyman. Since the battle was over, the crowd lost interest.

The priest peered at Peter over his spectacles. There was little face to see, mostly blood and dirt. "Ye best be wipin' off some of that mess.

Have ye a handkerchief?"

Peter could not stop an occasional sniffle while he went through his pockets. He found a ball of twine, a badly battered knife, and a few other items indispensable to a boy of twelve, but no handkerchief.

The man looked a bit rueful. "Ye'd not be havin' one, I suppose." He thrust a fat hand into one of his own pockets and brought forth a white and freshly laundered handkerchief of his own. "Here, ye'll have to use this."

Peter took it and mopped. The priest's laundress would not have recognized her own handiwork. When something that looked like a face began to emerge from behind the traces of battle, the priest turned to inspect the little dog, who was standing close by and eagerly watching.

"What did ye say that animal was?"

"A dog, sir." The tone suggested a mixture of surprise and indignation.

"A dog!" The reverend father stroked his chin thoughtfully—this seemed to be a habit of his. "A dog! Well, I'm glad to know at last. Many's the time I've seen him about the streets, but I could never be rightly sure what he was. What kind of a dog do ye call him?"

"His name's Brownie."

"That will do as well as any other, I presume. But what I mean is, what kind of a dog does he lay claim to be. He wouldn't be a mastiff, nor yet a St. Bernard, nor a . . ."

"I reckon he's all kinds," said his owner with an attempt at a smile.

"He appears to me like a descendant of all the craytures the Blessed Lord sent on the Ark with Noah. But he's got good, honest eyes and a cowlick, even if he don't kape it clane. And that's something. Come here, ye brute." He squatted down and held out a friendly hand.

Brownie hesitated, but like all dogs he had a sure instinct that told him who was a friend. He crossed over slowly and held his head down to be scratched. In a moment the little stub of a tail was jerking from side to side.

"Ye're a quare lookin' animal, there's no denyin' thot, but ye're one of God's craytures, and ye've a good character, I've no doubt." He rose to his feet. "And now—but I don't know yer name."

"Peter."

"Then, Peter, ye'd best be runnin' on home to yer mother so that she

13

can wash the face on ye and make ye fit to live in civilization again."

"I haven't got any mother, sir," answered the boy.

"Oh." There was a new note of tenderness in the man's voice. "Well, then, to whoever takes care of ye."

"I live with Mrs. Morris on Fourth near Spruce. My Pa's gone to Santa Fe, and she takes care of me. But Mr. Morris died last month, and she don't have much money. I want to go find my Pa. You're not goin' to Santa Fe, are you?" he added hopefully.

"No, I'm not, son, though I'd like to, to work there with His Reverence, the good Bishop Lamy. The Blessed Lord has given me my work to do here in St. Louis, and it's not for a poor Father like me to question His will. Well, ye're a brave lad, and ye put up a mighty good fight. The Lord bless ye!" He turned to go, but stopped to add, "And ye've got a good dog, too. Goodbye to you, Brownie." And the little man trotted off down the street.

Suddenly Peter became aware that he had not returned the borrowed handkerchief. He looked at it, a sodden mass of red and brown, clutched in his hand.

"Hey—Hey, Mister!" He raced after the retreating figure.

"Here's your handkerchief, sir."

The priest stopped and turned to wait for him.

"Here it is, sir. And—and thanks ever so much." He held it out.

The good father peered at it doubtfully over his glasses. "Yes, yes," he murmured, his hand back at his chin. "Yes, I see. I—I think ye'd best be kaping it. Ye might be nadin' it more than mesilf."

"I'll wash it, and return it," the boy said shyly.

"All right, son, if ye like. Bring it to the Parish House next to the Cathedral, and ask for Father Donahue. I'll be glad to see you again."

"You're sure you don't need it now?" The boy was still uncertain.

"Oh, yes, quite sure," the other added hastily. He looked at his property a little as if he were afraid it might be thrust into his hand and was off again down the sloping street.

Peter watched him in silence, and then slowly resumed his walk home. Brownie, sobered by his recent adventure, trotted sedately at his heels.

Chapter One

2

Mrs. Morris Does Not Approve

Mrs. Morris did not live in one of the large handsome residences on the fashionable part of Fourth Street, but as Peter had told Father Donahue, down near Spruce some blocks to the south. So when he and Brownie had climbed the hill to the fine new Courthouse, they still had a long way to go after turning left onto Fourth. But the evening was pleasant, and neither was in any particular hurry to get home. They walked slowly along the broad street, stopping often. The dog sampled each new smell with a twitching nose; the boy was absorbed in his own thoughts and oblivious to the smiles with which the passersby regarded his battle-scarred face and bloody shirt.

But all walks must end, and at last they came to a halt in front of a small, dark red brick house on the west side of the street. It was not a very cheerful looking building, especially now that the woodwork was sadly in need of paint. Further, the grass in the thin strip of yard had withered in the summer heat, but if either boy or dog were aware of these facts, he did not show it. Peter swung open the gate of the low picket fence that separated the yard from the sidewalk and held it open for Brownie. The two then followed a dingy brick walk around to the backyard. There Brownie, once more on home territory, ran off on three legs to investigate rat holes and buried bones that had been neglected during his absence. Peter slowly climbed the back steps to the kitchen door and went inside.

He found preparations for supper under way. Mrs. Morris was busy at a table by the window cutting biscuits out of a slab of dough, while Eliza, a pig-tailed child of nine, was perched on top of a nearby chair shelling peas. Mrs. Morris was too busy to notice anything unusual. She spoke without even looking up, her voice sounding tired and just-ready-to-be-cross. "Peter run down to Mr. Perrier's and get a pound of sugar. There's a dime on the shelf."

He started across the room to pick up the money, but Eliza's eyes were popping out of her head and her beribboned pigtails were shaking violently. "What's happened to your face? Mama, look at his face!"

Peter tried to ignore this revelation, but there was no use.

Mrs. Morris put down her biscuit-cutter and ordered him to come to her to be inspected. She opened her mouth wider than it had ever been and then shut it very tight, only to open it again at once.

"Peter Blair, what have you been doing this time?"

He hung his head. "Nuthin'."

Eliza left her chair and the peas and hurried over to see the details.

"Mama, look at his shirt. It's got blood all over it!"

"I see," replied her mother grimly. "Now, tell me what you did."

"I—just had a fight."

"A fight!" She was plainly exasperated. "Haven't I troubles enough but you must run about town getting into all sorts of fights and—it seems to me you might have a little gratitude and think of me sometimes."

Peter flushed and looked up. "I don't get into so many fights. Anyway, this one was all right. A boy kicked Brownie." This was obviously ample justification so far as he was concerned. He didn't think it necessary to mention the fact that the kick had missed.

"Brownie!" His defense had evidently done no good. "That dog! It seems to me that half the time you get into trouble that brute's at the bottom of it."

"I couldn't just go and let him be kicked, could I? Had to protect him, didn't I?"

"You wouldn't have had to protect him if you didn't have him. This is what comes of my letting you keep stray animals, as if I had food enough for my own children! And who's going to wash your shirt and mend it, I'd like to know?" She had to stop a moment for breath. "Well enough

I do know. I'll have to—on top of all the other things I have to do."

This time Peter's eyes did fill up with tears, and he had to bite his lip before he could answer. "I'm sorry, Mrs. Morris. Honest, I am. But I had to. Brownie's my best friend, and . . ."

"Your best friend!" It was evident that everything he said was only making matters worse. "Your best friend! I like that! Does Brownie give you a home and food? Does Brownie wear his fingers to the bone mending your clothes and darning your stockings? Of all the ingratitude!"

"I . . ."

"Don't say another word. Eliza, you call Belle and tell her she'll have to leave her lesson and come bake the biscuits. Peter, you come with me."

She marched out of the kitchen and led the way upstairs to a small closet in a front bedroom where the shelves were lined with all sorts and sizes of bottles and jars containing household remedies.

"Now stand still here by the window," she ordered, "and don't move even if it does hurt." Mrs. Morris's tongue was sharper than she knew. She dipped a washrag into the large china pitcher on the washstand and proceeded to mop the battered face. There was some question whether there was more blood or dirt on it. Peter winced, but did not cry out.

"I got some of it off with this," he murmured as he produced the priest's handkerchief.

"Good gracious, where did you get that?" Mrs. Morris stopped to examine the piece of linen, at least as well as she could without actually taking hold of it.

"A sort o' priest gave it to me. He said his name was Donahue, and he lives by the Cathedral. He was the one who pulled us apart."

"And he gave you his handkerchief? Well, he must be a Christian man." She gave an extra hard rub, which drew an "Ouch!" from Peter. "Now wait," she went on, "till I rub it with this arnica. It'll take the soreness out."

If it really was the intent of the arnica to take soreness out, Peter's expression and outcries were certainly a poor advertisement. However, at last, the treatment was over, and he was released to go wash his hands and change his shirt while Mrs. Morris returned to the kitchen to finish the preparations for supper.

It was no wonder that her patience was sometimes tried. She had suddenly been left a widow with very little income and had, not only her own three children, but an outsider as well to provide for. Peter's mother had died when he was little more than a baby. He could not remember her at all. After her death, an aunt had come to keep house for his father and take care of the child. But then two years ago, she too had passed away, and Peter and his father had been left alone. Mr. Blair, overwhelmed by the changes in his life, had turned the boy over to the wife of his best friend and gone West to make his fortune in the former Mexican territories that had been conquered recently by the United States.

At first Peter had been no burden to the Morrises. His father had given Mr. Morris quite a bit of money to pay for Peter's board, and he had just taken his place in the household. But the money had in time given out, and his father had sent no more—in fact, Peter did not hear from him for months at a time—and then Mr. Morris's business had failed. Mrs. Morris's situation got even worse—Mr. Morris came down with pneumonia and died about a month before Peter's fight with the big boy. The widow was hard put to make ends meet and, because of worry and grief, was not as good-natured and patient as she had once been. Yet she was never really unkind and continued to take just as good care of her ward as of her own brood.

It was not very long after Peter had washed—he took extra pains to make himself reasonably presentable, at least in front of his ears and above his neck—that he heard Eliza's shrill voice shouting, "Supper's ready! Supper's ready!" He went downstairs, though none too certain of the reception he would receive.

The Morris dining room was not large and, when the whole family was assembled around the table, there was not much space left to move about. When he came in, everyone was there, and, except for his uncertainty as to what was likely to happen next, he found the prospects pleasing. Mrs. Morris was just putting a platter containing a steaming pork roast in front of her place, and his adventures of the afternoon had given him an appetite which later events had not destroyed. The boiled potatoes also looked good. Belle, a rather pale-faced, solemn looking girl of fifteen, was bringing them in as he entered. The peas Eliza had shelled were already on the table, and the biscuits Mrs. Morris had been cutting out when he came home had grown into great, fluffy brown-crusted affairs which made his mouth water as he looked at them. Having settled the meat in its proper place, the mother took her seat and the children lost no time in getting into theirs. Belle, as the oldest of the children, sat opposite her, John, a chubby, red-haired youngster of six was on her right, and Eliza sat stiffly on her left. Peter's seat was between the two girls, and he slipped into it silently, hoping that the past had been forgotten. It was obvious, however, from the curious expressions of the children that it had not. But before anything could be said, Mrs. Morris spoke.

"Eliza, you may ask the blessing this evening."

The little girl blinked and then quickly rattled off the familiar words, while the others sat with their heads bowed, but John, at least, with furtively roving eyes.

The grace was no sooner disposed of than John cried out, "Peter, tell us about your fight. Who was the boy? Did you wallop him? Did . . ."

But his mother cut him short. "That's enough. Don't ask about the fight. I don't want to hear anything more about it. Peter, don't you tell him. You set a very bad example, and the less said about it, the better."

"Well, I don't care! I think it was noble of him to protect Brownie!" Eliza, of all the children, was Peter's champion and ally. Now her voice was shrill with indignation. But she was quelled by her mother's frozen stare, and her eyes fell.

"If you say anything more like that, you'll go to bed right away without any supper. Peter was a bad boy. Wait till you're spoken to."

After this there was silence. Mrs. Morris served the roast, and Belle helped the others to potatoes and peas. Their eyes were fixed on their plates, except for stolen glances at one another, until their mother decided to question them about their schoolwork. The answers were given briefly, consisting mostly of "Yes, ma'ams" and "No ma'ams." Plainly they all recognized storm signals and knew from experience that the safest course was to say and, if possible, do nothing. One thing was certain—none of them noticed that their mother's piece of pork was the smallest and most gristly on the table.

But the ordeal was not over.

"Peter, why aren't you eating your meat? Perhaps it isn't good enough for you."

"Yes, ma'am, it's very good."

"Then why don't you eat it?"

Silence.

"Then why don't you eat it? Answer my question."

"I'm savin' it."

"Saving it! What for?"

It was almost impossible to get an answer out of the boy. "What are you saving it for?" She spoke slowly and emphatically.

After a long pause, "For Brownie."

This was the last straw. "For Brownie. For Brown— ! Peter Blair, have you the impudence to sit there and tell me that you're saving a piece of meat I bought and cooked myself for a common dirty cur dog?"

"He's not common, and he's not dirty!" Peter's defense was more ardent than correct.

Mrs. Morris's voice rose. "You wicked, ungrateful boy! How can you sit there and look me in the face while you say things like that. Here I am buying food and depriving my own children and myself of the necessities of life, and you go and waste them on a dog!"

"It's not wasting 'em!" There was one subject over which Peter would always fight. "He's got to live, hasn't he?"

"No!" The answer was forceful enough. "He does not have to live—at least in this house. And he isn't going to. You get rid of him tomorrow. I'm not feeding dogs."

"I won't." Peter was on his feet now.

"You won't? Then I will, and I don't care how."

The boy was trembling all over. "We'll go, both of us. I'll go and take him with me."

"Nonsense, you'll do as I say. Your father left you here, and here you'll stay till he comes for you."

"No, ma'am. You can't stop me. I'll run away. I won't let you hurt Brownie! I won't let you! I won't let anybody hurt him!" The boy threw his napkin down on the table, and pushed back his chair. He was so frantic that he scarcely knew what he said or did.

Mrs. Morris too was on the verge of tears. "Peter . . ."

Tinkle! Tinkle! From the kitchen came the feeble note of a small bell attached by a cord to a knob on the front door. Instantly the woman was still, struggling to get control of herself.

"There's someone at the front door. Be still now. You don't want people to hear you crying."

"I'm not crying," the boy muttered.

"Well, be still. Belle, you're the only one who's fit to be seen. You go see who's there." Mrs. Morris began to pat her hair and brush the crumbs from her black skirt.

Belle slid out of the room as if glad to escape, and the other children held their breaths, all but Peter, who stood with his back to his chair glowering at the wall.

*The first thing he saw when he opened
the front door was the beard.*

3

Peter Makes Big Plans

They were all silent for what seemed an eternity, but finally they heard the front door open and then a heavy male voice asking questions. They could not make out the words. Belle was back in a minute, wide-eyed and pale.

"It's somebody to see Peter," she whispered. "A great big man with a long beard. He's awful funny lookin'!"

Peter jumped. He turned to look at her, while the rest all fixed their eyes on him as though he could solve the mystery.

"Maybe it's that priest," suggested Mrs. Morris.

"No, ma'am. He didn't have a beard."

"Where did you leave him, Belle?"

"Out on the porch," answered the girl.

"Out on the porch!" Her mother was scandalized. "That's no place to leave a caller. Peter, go see who he is and what he wants. But first come here. You aren't fit to be seen. What would people think of me?"

Reluctantly the boy crossed to her and submitted to emergency improvements, including the rubbing off of some dirt with the corner of a handkerchief moistened in Mrs. Morris's mouth, an operation he manfully resented, but was compelled to endure.

"Now go—and mind your manners."

Peter started for the hall.

The first thing he saw when he opened the front door was the beard. It certainly was a big one, brown and bushy. Although beards were especially popular among the trappers he had seen on the levee unloading their furs, he was sure he had never seen one to equal this. It was not only long, reaching well down onto the man's chest, but it was also broad—Peter would have guessed a foot wide if he had been asked. At first the boy was spellbound by the sight, but in a second he remembered himself and looked above the beard at two little eyes, strangely small in contrast, that were peering out above the beard and from under the shelter of a huge felt hat.

"Well, son," came a deep voice out through the beard, "have you had a good enough look?"

"I beg your pardon." Peter stammered. "I . . . I . . ." He could not think of anything more to say.

"Are you Peter Blair?" the voice asked and there was something about the sound that the boy liked.

"Yes, sir. Who are you?"

"I'm old Seth Bowen, and I've come from Santa Fe"—only he pronounced it Santa Fee.

Peter drew in his breath sharply. "Santa Fe?" He could hardly repeat the name. He went hot and cold all over at the same time and had to grip the doorknob to hold steady.

"I reckon you've heard of that there place, young'un. I've brought you word from yer Pa."

"H-how . . . is . . . he?" The words were almost inaudible.

"Wal," the man went on, "last time I seen him he wuz able to sit up and take nourishment. What you lookin' so scared fer, son? There ain't nuthin' wrong with yer Pa. He's as healthy a man as ever I see, but he's kinda curious to hear somethin' 'bout a little rooster he left in St. Louis. So long's I was a-comin' here anyhow, I 'lowed I'd have a look at you. And you ain't half bad to look at either fer a city-boy, 'cept you look's if you'd been chawed up by a varmint of some sort."

"Peter, ask your friend to come in and sit down." Mrs. Morris was standing in the hall with all three children gaping from behind her skirts at the mysterious stranger.

He was ready enough to obey this command. "Won't you come in?" he asked politely.

Chapter Three

"Don't mind if I do," said the visitor, removing the huge hat with a sweeping gesture. "Yer servant, ma'am." He made a bow to Mrs. Morris. Despite the roughness of his appearance and the strangeness of his attire, there was a kind of dignity and grace about his manner, and there was deference in every sentence he addressed to his hostess.

"Let's go in the parlor," she said. "Peter, you run in and light the lamp. John, take the gentleman's hat. Right this way, sir."

"Old Seth," as he called himself, was probably the biggest thing that had ever been in the Morris house—and undoubtedly the strangest. As soon as Peter succeeded in lighting the oil lamp with his trembling fingers, they all got a better look at Seth and his outfit. The youngsters were unable to conceal their curiosity. The upper part of his body was covered by a huge shapeless garment of buckskin that was decorated in every possible place with long fringes of the same material. There was fringe about the bottom, fringe along each sleeve from the wrist to the shoulder, fringe under the pockets, and matted masses of it all over each shoulder. It even ran down the seams of the trousers, which were somewhat tighter fitting than the coat. Now that he had taken his hat off, the children could see an uncombed mop of thick brown hair covering the top of his head and falling down to his massive shoulders. The whole outfit seemed rather unsuited to a warm May evening, but, if it were too heavy, the owner showed no sign of it.

"Ma'am," he said, "it's a long time since I been in a house like yers. And it's a sight for sore eyes. But I'm 'most afraid to turn 'round."

"You needn't be, I'm sure, sir," replied Mrs. Morris. "Everything we have is very simple." She directed him to a chair by the mantel, but he had his eyes on something else.

"I want to see this young wild-cat here," he said, looking searchingly at Peter, who, having at last lit the lamp—burning his fingers in the act—was staring at him in awe. "Come here, young'un. Where'd you get all them claw marks on your face?"

"He was in a fight," John volunteered.

"A fight, huh?" The big man drew the boy toward him, placing two huge paws on his shoulders and peering down at him with eyes that Peter felt were boring holes right through his skull. "Did you get licked or did you lick the other fellow?"

"Somebody made us stop, a sort o' priest."

"That's too bad. A fight's no good unless somebody comes out on top." He turned to Mrs. Morris. "Oughtn't never stop boys when they get into a fight. It's the best exercise in the world. Gives 'em grit too." He turned back to Peter. "What'd you fight about?"

"The other boy kicked his dog." Eliza wanted to get into the conversation too.

"Wal, wal!" exclaimed the visitor, "that's better still. Fit fer yer dog, did you? Yer Pa'll be proud to hear that. Ma'am," and again he addressed himself to Mrs. Morris, "there ain't no better sign of a fine character in a boy than love fer a dog or a hoss. I wouldn't give a copper cent fer a young'un who wouldn't take up fer his dog. If Peter here fit fer his'n till he got hurt—and 'pears to me like he did—he deserved a extra big dinner an' all the pie he could tuck away. I hope you give it to him."

This was a hard moment for Mrs. Morris. With three small pairs of eyes fastened on her—Peter, flushed with embarrassment and pleasure, was staring at the empty fireplace—she was completely confused and at a loss for a word.

Eliza drew a deep breath and was about to report recent proceedings, but she remembered that in the natural course of events "company" did not stay forever, and she wisely held her peace.

It was now Mrs. Morris's turn to feel that the eyes were boring straight through her, and she stammered in reply. "Well, I . . . I . . . I never thought of it that way, Mr. Bowen. I daresay you're right, but—it's hard being a widow woman with four children to raise and little money put away. I'm afraid I am cross at times."

"A widow woman!" the caller exclaimed. "Abel never told me that."

"He doesn't know it," she went on, wiping her eyes. "My husband died five weeks ago tomorrow, and . . ." The poor woman was unable to continue.

"I'm right sorry to hear it, ma'am. And Abel will be too." He fumbled in a trouser pocket and produced a small cotton bag tied shut with a thong of deerskin. "He give me this to hand to yer husband, but I cal'ate now it belongs to you—and to Peter here." And he held it out to her.

But she made no move to take it. "What is it?" she asked.

"If Abel told me rightly—and he's an honest man—thar's a hunderd dollars fer you, ma'am, and twenty-five fer the boy."

They all gasped in amazement. Seeing that no one made a move, Seth undid the knot with a dexterity that was surprising in such enormous fingers, and, crossing to a table, spilled out a glittering heap of gold coins that jingled and clinked as they fell. The children's eyes nearly popped out of their heads, and their mother stood, wide-eyed, her hand over her open mouth.

John was the first to find his tongue. "Is all that gold?"

"That's what it is, sonny. An' there's plenty more where that came from."

One by one, the youngsters stepped forward to feel it. Mrs. Morris's knees gave away and, to the consternation of the caller, she sank into a chair, weeping violently.

Seth did not know which way to turn or what to say. "Ma'am, I didn't reckon . . . You mustn't take on this way. I've got some more here, an' I'll . . ."

"No, no!" she exclaimed, getting hold of herself. "It's not that. There's plenty there, more than plenty. It's just that I've been so worried. My poor husband left me so little, and now . . ." Again she was unable to go on. But in a moment, she regained control of herself and rose to her feet. "I can't tell you how much I thank you and Mr. Blair. I declare I've been so upset I've never even asked you to have a seat. I don't know what's become of my manners. Please sit down, Mr.—er—Bowen."

"Call me 'Uncle Seth,' ma'am, I ain't used to fancy handles." He looked about uncertainly. "I don't figger I better sit on one o' yer purty chairs. I'm afeard they wouldn't last long under an old ruffian like me."

"I think they're strong enough." Mrs. Morris was trying, under difficult circumstances, to be a perfect hostess.

"Their legs is too spindly. I'll jest set here on the ground. Seems more natural anyhow." And lowering his great bulk to the floor, he settled himself comfortably before the fireplace, which he almost completely blocked from view. The children, overcoming their awe, crowded closer and were soon seated in a circle, watching each move he made and hanging on every word he spoke.

"Have you just come from Santa Fe?" It was Eliza who found her voice first.

27

"Yes, honey. Jest come down from Independence this mornin'. Caught the Prairie Rose there an' come down the river in record time."

Mrs. Morris glanced uneasily at the gold on the table. "Mr. Blair must be a very rich man to be able to spare such a large sum."

Uncle Seth pondered the question before answering. "No, Abel don't live like a king, ma'am. Plenty of fellows have made their piles when nobody wuz lookin' close. But he ain't that kind of a man. You'll never have to be ashamed o' yer Pa, Peter." It had never occurred to Peter that such a thing was possible.

"What kind of business is Mr. Blair in?" asked Mrs. Morris.

"He's clerk in a good store on the Plaza. Me an' my pardner are carryin' some stuff out fer him to sell."

Peter could not help feeling a bit let down. Clerking in a store was not as glamorous as trapping beaver and fighting Indians. But he said nothing.

"How long did it take you to make the trip from Santa Fe to Independence?" Mrs. Morris inquired politely.

"'Bout six weeks, ma'am. We traveled light—didn't have no wagons to slow us down."

"How far is it?"

"Wal, I ain't never counted the miles myself. They ain't got no mileposts along the Trail. But they say it's about eight hundred if you go by the dry way and quite a bit better'n that if you go over the mountains. Considerable of a trip either way, but it ain't ever seemed long to me somehow. It's wonderful country, ma'am, when it ain't too cold er too hot, and thet's most o' the time."

"Have you ever seen any Indians?" John's voice was vibrant with curiosity.

"Have I ever seen any Injuns?" The big man eyed the child with amusement. "Do I see you now? I reckon I've seen a good many more than you've ever seen white folks. An' some of 'em wished they'd never seen me, I cal'ate. An' some of 'em come pretty close to makin' Old Seth wish he hadn't seen 'em. But I'm here, and they ain't. So I can't complain."

"Do you mean you've killed some?" John's eyes were like saucers.

"Umhh, I figgered that mebbe they wuz anxious to see what the Happy Huntin' Grounds looked like. So I kinda give 'em a shove in that direction. But I wuz fergettin'."

Here he paused while he thrust his right hand deep into one of the fringed pockets in his coat. The pocket was big, but so was his hand, and it was sometime before he succeeded in extricating it. When he did, it was gripping something that resembled a small horse's tail, long black strands of hair attached at one end to something brown. The whole party leaned forward eagerly to see what it was.

"Here, sonny, wear this in yer belt till you c'n get you one fer yerself." And he tossed it to Peter, who was sitting cross-legged beside the table. The boy took it in his hands and studied it. Suddenly he began to turn pale.

"What . . . is . . . it? Is it a . . . scalp?" He seemed to have trouble getting the last word out.

"One o' them Injuns left it behind him when he went to the Happy Huntin' Grounds."

Peter looked a trifle sick, but he did not let the scalp fall from his grasp. Mrs. Morris gasped and gripped the arms of her chair with both hands. The two girls backed away, their eyes glued on the ghastly trophy. Only John crawled closer.

Peter wet his lips. "I never saw one before," he murmured.

"Old Seth" was quite unconscious of the effect of his offering. "Take it to school with you and show it to the boys. They'll all envy you. Maybe after that," and there was a twinkle in his beady little eyes, "you won't get yer face all clawed up agin."

"Thank you, sir. I will." But as soon as he saw his friend looking at someone else, he reached up and put his present on the table where it lay under the lamp in striking contrast to the glittering gold coins. After that, Mrs. Morris could not bring herself to look in that direction. It was some time before she could regain her composure.

"Did you get it on your way here this time? Tell us all about it." John wanted to know all the details. "I didn't know white people scalped Indians. I just thought Indians scalped white folks."

Seth laughed cheerfully. "What's sauce fer the goose is sauce fer the gander," he quoted, much to the mystification of John, who could not see what geese had to do with Indians. "It's a long story. Mebbe yer Ma would rather I didn't start in on it."

Mrs. Morris, having undergone several shocks already, was not at all certain, but she thought it would not be polite to say no. So she compromised by saying it was all right, but that it was John's bedtime, and he must say good night. This ruling was greeted by a yell from John. He put up such a fight that the poor woman didn't have the strength to resist and finally consented to let him remain, though warning him first that he was sure to have dreadful dreams. That matter settled, the children once more closed in on the storyteller, and he began.

"Wal," he commenced, shifting one foot to a more comfortable position and clasping his hands behind his head, "it all happened at Pawnee Rock. We'd come up from Santa Fe by the Cimarron Route and crossed the Arkansas near the old Mexican line. The river wuz pretty full and we'd o' had plenty of trouble on our hands if we'd had any wagons, but, as 'twas we just had our mules, an' they could swim pretty good. So we got across an' no harm done in particular."

"How many of you were there?" It was Peter who asked.

"Just three—Bud Porter, Pete Jones, and me. That's not much of a party when you're travelin' through Injun country, but we wuz all old hands and had plenty o' powder; so we figgered we could take care of ourselves. Traders who'd just come over the Trail from the East hadn't reported seein' many Injuns and said things wuz pretty quiet; so we didn't worry none.

"Wal," he resumed, "we did see couple o' Injuns near McNees' Crossing, but they didn't bother us none, even if they wuz Comanches. I reckon they thought there wuzn't enough of 'em. They never likes to strike 'nless they're 'bout five to one. Wanta steal horses and anything else they can get their hands on. We got rid of 'em an' thought things'd still be quiet north o' the river, on account of thar wuz soldiers at Fort Atkinson. We didn't hev no trouble at the ford 'count o' the Fort. But in 'bout two hours we noticed thet thar wuzn't no buffalo grazin' near the river, an' thet didn't look so good. Why not, sonny? 'Cause buffalo don' like Injuns an' keeps out o' their way when they kin. This made us keep our weather eyes open.

"Wal them buffalo knowed their bizness. Jest after we'd crossed

Pawnee Fork, we seen a Pawnee scout lookin' us over, an' thet meant we wuz in fer trouble."

"What's Pawnee Fork?" John wanted to know all the answers.

"It's a lil ole crick thet sort o' doubles back on itself, jest out o' cussedness, I reckon, so folks'll hev' to cross it twice. Its banks is slipp'ry as—is slipp'ry as all tarnation after a rain. Wal, lucky fer us, it didn't start to rain till after we wuz across. Thet wuz when thet Pawnee brave got sight of us. We wuz lucky thet it rained though, or I mightn't be settin' here borin' you all with my yarns.

"We decided to hit fer Pawnee Rock. We c'd be sure them Injuns wouldn't attack us afore daylight. Their favorite time is jest afore sun-up, an' we cal'ated we c'd reach the Rock by then. We didn't hev fur to go— less 'n ten miles—but I wuz bothered 'cause Ash Crick wuz in the way, an' its banks is purty steep. But we didn't hev no trouble there. The way we run them critters down one side an' up the other wuz wild. The furtherer we went, the faster we made 'em go. We hed to look about us too so's not to pass the Rock in the dark. Comin' at it from the east, nobody c'd miss it, but it rises up so gradual from the west an' north, we jest mightn't notice it. We purty near did miss it too, only a flash o' lightnin' showed us we wuz there. Wuz we glad! We figgered we c'd hold off all the Injuns thar wuz in thet party."

Even Mrs. Morris was excited now, "Why did you think you'd be safe there?" she asked. "What is Pawnee Rock?"

"It's a great big rock—or mebbe you'd call it a small hill, ma'am— right out in the middle o' the plains on the left bank o' the Arkansas River. The side to'rd the river an' the one facin' the east is real steep; the other two is sort o' gradual. I reckon it's least as high as this house o' yourn, mebbe a good bit higher. It makes a kind o' natural fort, and, wal, there's been lot's a fights there, ma'am. Injuns 'gainst Injuns, and Injuns 'gainst whites. Three o' my pardners has turned up their toes there, one time or another. But I didn't have no plans 'bout turnin' mine up, an' we got ready fer whatever wuz comin', an' we was purty shore that would be horse-thievin' Pawnees.

"We tethered all the mules in the middle of the top, an' there's lots o' room up there. There wuz plenty o' good grass too; so they wuz quiet.

Then Pete an' me lay down on our bellies an' watch the low sides o' the rock, and Bud took care o' the south. Fer a long time we didn't hear nary a sound—not till it began to git daylight. Then, just as soon as it wuz bright enough fer you to begin to see things, come a yell, an' here comes about fifteen half-naked Injuns runnin' up the hill toward me an' Pete. They wuz shootin' bows an' arrows, and them arrows fell all 'round us like hail. We wuz glad o' that, 'cause it showed they didn't hev guns. We held our fire till we could see good. Then we let loose, and two of 'em fell right over in their tracks. That showed 'em we meant business, and they took to cover in a hurry. Never did see a Injun who wuz careless 'bout lettin' the other feller git a drop on 'im. Bud hollered over to know how we wuz gittin' 'long. We answered that we wuz doin' nicely, thanks, an' just then Pete let out a yell. I looked at him, an' there wuz a arrow stickin' out o' his shoulder like it'd sprouted there."

"Oooh!" Eliza drew a deep breath and covered her mouth with her hand to keep from screaming out loud.

Old Seth was plainly enjoying his story and its reception. "Just then," he went on, "the Injuns began screechin' and starts up the Rock agin. They thought one of us wuz dead an' this wuz a good time to kill the rest. But they didn't know old Pete. He plumb fergot all about thet arrow and kep' on pumpin' lead into their hides. Soon's they found that out, they scuttled back to cover behind some cedars at the foot o' the hill. Thet is, all but one of 'em. He didn't scuttle nowhere. I bored a hole clean through his forehead, an' he's the gentleman whose scalp lock is decoratin' yer parlor table at this minute." He motioned toward the table, and Mrs. Morris shuddered.

"What did you do then?" John was the family questioner.

"Jest set tight, an' thanked the Lord fer thet rain. A favorite trick o' them is to shoot fire-arrers up an' burn the people out. But they can't do thet when the grass is wet, an' it shore wuz wet thet night. Thet's what saved our hides."

"God moves in a mysterious way," murmured Mrs. Morris piously.

Seth looked at her and tugged at his beard. "Yes, ma'am, He does," he responded.

Chapter Three

But John had another question to ask. "What became of the other Indians?"

"Oh, they vamoosed. They didn't like what had happened to their friend there, an' I reckon they hurried home with the bad news. We made a early start too. But first, I collected thet trophy fer Peter—can't call ye 'Pete,' fer my pardner has claim to thet name . . ."

Peter would have liked to say that he hated "Pete," but he didn't think it would be polite to do so.

"Thet's whar it come from, son." He laid a large hand kindly on the boy's knee. "If folks ask ye whut it is, jest tell 'em it's the scalp lock of a Pawnee brave."

The story completed, the visitor rose to his feet with an agility surprising for one of his bulk. "I reckon I'd best be sayin' good night, ma'am. I've sure enjoyed my visit. I'll tell Peter's pa he's fit as a fiddle. I'll tell 'im 'bout thet fight, too—an' he'll be mighty proud. Good night to ye, ma'am."

"What became of the arrow?" Of course it was John who asked.

"What arrow?"

"The one in Mr. Pete's shoulder."

This was obviously a detail of no importance. "Oh, we jest jerked it out. Pete never even kep' it."

The children were all on their feet. Peter stepped forward, tense with excitement.

"Mr. . . . Mr. Seth," he began.

"Call me 'Uncle Seth.'"

"Well . . . Uncle Seth . . . when . . . when are you startin' back?"

"Oh, I reckon . . . lemme see. Today's Thursday. Thar's a good boat goin' up the river next Tuesday. I sort o' figgered on goin' then."

"I want to go with you."

This announcement was breathtaking. The children gasped.

"Peter!" exclaimed Mrs. Morris. "Don't talk nonsense."

The boy turned on her fiercely. "It ain't nonsense! I want to go. Please take me, Uncle Seth. Please!"

"Why, sonny," the man looked in bewilderment from the child to the woman.

33

"Don't listen to him," she exclaimed. "It's out of the question."

"It isn't! It isn't! It isn't!" Peter cried passionately. "Other boys have gone, lots of 'em. There's no reason why I can't."

"You'd be in Mr. Seth's way."

"No, I wouldn't. Would I, Uncle Seth? I wouldn't!"

"Your father left you with us to be sent to school. I couldn't think of letting you . . ."

"I don't need no more schooling. I'm twelve years old. Uncle Seth, you didn't go to school after you were twelve, did you?"

The man scratched his head in embarrassment. "Wal . . . I . . . I wouldn't want you to take me fer no example."

"Don't, Peter, don't" wailed Eliza. "The Indians would shoot arrows into you!"

"No, they wouldn't," he replied hotly. "I c'n shoot. Least, I—can learn. Uncle Seth'll teach me. Won't you? Oh, please, say you'll let me go. I want to see my Pa. I want to see him. It's been more'n a year and . . ."

"He would never consent," declared Mrs. Morris.

"He would too!" Peter stamped his foot. "How do you know he wouldn't? He wants to see me just like I want to see him. I know he does. And I'm goin'. If Uncle Seth won't take me, somebody else will. I'm just in the way here—and cost you money. You said so yourself this evening. You said you were going to hurt Brownie."

"Peter!" Here Mrs. Morris burst into tears and sank back into her chair.

The other children stood about, their mouths open wide. They had never seen Peter like this before. Seth Bowen stood in silence, too, but nothing would stem the flow of words from the boy. He argued. He begged. He threatened. His whole body was trembling with emotion. Mrs. Morris dared not try to quiet him. She merely sat in her chair and wept.

"You know my Pa wants me!"

The man began to weaken. "Wal . . . I . . . reckon he does," Seth stammered. "He shore talks about you a lot."

"You see!" cried the boy as if that had clinched the argument.

In the end there was no resisting him. Defense after defense crumbled.

He had an answer for every objection. Finally Mrs. Morris, exhausted and secretly a trifle relieved, gave her consent if Uncle Seth were willing. He was. The boy had won the man's warm heart completely, and at last he said: "Wal, Peter, it looks like you an' me's to be pardners." He held out a huge, calloused hand into which the boy thrust his small one. The man and boy looked each other in the eye for a moment, and then at the same moment they both smiled. "An' that's that."

Half an hour later when the old plainsman tramped down the front porch steps, the bargain had been sealed, and it had been arranged that Peter was to meet him on the levee the following Tuesday in time to catch the Queen of the Forest. There had been one bad moment that had caused Peter to pale. How about Brownie? Determined as he was to go, no force on earth would part him from his beloved friend. But Seth had said Brownie would be welcome. The little dog had been brought in and duly presented, politely offering a brown paw to his new ally. With that fear allayed, the Road to the West was open.

That night a new moon shone through a large window onto a bed where a small tow-haired boy lay dreaming of Indians and prairie-fires— a tousle-headed little dog curled up on the cover by his feet.

35

Peter Makes Big Plans

4

The Great Adventure Begins

Peter would not remember much that happened during the next few days. He was so excited that he lived in a kind of trance, and the experiences of the following weeks were so thrilling that they wiped his memory clean of the trivial incidents that preceded them.

When he awoke the morning after Uncle Seth's visit, he forgot for a moment the events of the evening before, but in a few seconds the recollection burst upon him, and he was out of bed in a flash. He did not usually waste much time washing, and this morning he paid less attention to it than usual. In an incredibly short time he was out of his nightshirt and into his patched trousers and faded tan shirt. He almost forgot to go through the formality of washing his face, but then imagined Mrs. Morris's reaction at the breakfast table if he did not.

He thought it would be just as well to be able to say that he had done his duty; so he ran back to his room, poured a little water into the china washbasin, and splashed a few drops onto his freckled cheeks. "After all," he thought, "I really washed my face yesterday afternoon and won't have to do it again after Tuesday."

A minute later he was in the kitchen, and Brownie was making his morning rounds of the yard. Peter was not certain what Mrs. Morris's mood would be, and habit made him a bit wary, even though he knew he was soon to pass from under her control. But he found her very quiet— he escaped without a single reprimand. He could not know it, but the poor woman had had a bad night. Peter's public declaration that she had complained of the money he had cost her, especially coming as it did after the gift from his father, had mortified her. Her conscience was pinching her more than it really needed to. It was troubling her still more that she had consented to his going to Santa Fe. She was sure he would never reach his destination alive and find his father. It was she, not John, who dreamed about Indians, and every time she thought of the Pawnee scalp under the lamp on her parlor table, she shook till the bed rattled. And, most of all, she could not rid herself of what she considered a criminal feeling of relief that her burden was to be lightened. So she reserved her sharp words for her own children and filled Peter with pancakes and molasses. Once she thought, "Suppose he eats so much he gets sick and can't go." With a sense of guilt, she repeated this thought to him. He instantly dropped his well-loaded fork and left the table.

Of course, there were preparations to be made. Most of them seemed quite unnecessary to Peter, but they were, in fact, extremely simple. Mrs. Morris went over his small stock of clothing with great care and devoted a substantial amount of time and thread to repairing damages. She also insisted on wasting, so at least it seemed to him, a lot of money on finery. After all, who but Indians and traders would see him? But she was firm. Worst of all, she returned from one of her shopping expeditions with a large carpetbag covered with yellow roses displayed against a red background. His indignation was great, but it was useless to protest. His meager belongings—shirts, handkerchiefs, an extra pair of pants, stockings, toothbrush, knife, fork and spoon, and three nightshirts—all went into it. Imagine such things on the Santa Fe Trail! He secretly resolved to throw them all overboard as soon as the Queen of the Forest was out of sight of the levee.

He derived quite a bit of satisfaction, however, from the attitude of the other children. The word spread rapidly that he was going to cross the plains, and he found himself looked up to with a new respect. Boys who had hitherto honored him with little or no attention now sought him out and pressed upon him such gifts as broken knives and assorted nails. The little girls regarded him as a sort of combination Kit Carson and Josiah Gregg, marveling at his great courage. As for Eliza, she was fairly goggle-eyed and developed a bad habit of dropping whatever she might be holding while she stared at him with her mouth wide open. If the time of his departure had been delayed, she would surely have starved, because practically every spoonful of food that started for her mouth was turned upside down and lost before it reached its destination. In her efforts to wait upon her hero, she constantly got in his way, but Peter was too blissful to be cross.

Of course, the Pawnee scalp got the most attention. It was exhibited everywhere and admired by all the boys. The girls could not quite bring themselves to touch it, though they advanced cautious fingers toward it, only to draw them back with squeals of fright. All of this made Peter feel very superior. In fact, there were moments when he found himself almost believing that it had been he who had separated the black hair from its original owner. He wore it on his belt, but this was too much for Mrs. Morris, and it had to come off and go into his pocket whenever he entered the house.

On Monday, the day before his scheduled departure, Mrs. Morris called him and produced Father Donahue's handkerchief, once again as white and neatly pressed as when the little priest had lent it to Peter. She instructed him to return it to its owner and be sure to thank him. Off he marched along Fourth Street with Brownie by his side and the snowy square of linen clutched in his fist, which Mrs. Morris had made him scrub with unusual thoroughness before he set out. When he reached Walnut Street and turned east, he saw a familiar squat figure in a black cassock climbing the steps to the Cathedral door under the single pointed tower. He was afraid that the priest would disappear through the door before he could attract his attention; so he raced down the street shouting excitedly. Brownie added several loud yips to help.

"Father Donahue! Father Donahue!"

The plump little clergyman turned in surprise. So did several well-dressed ladies who were also going up the steps.

The future plainsman was out of breath by the time he reached the Cathedral. "I . . . I . . . I've . . . got . . . your handkerchief—all washed and clean," he panted. Father Donahue stopped and waited, his fat red hand clutching his prayer book. "It's all clean. Mrs. Morris . . ." But in his hurry Peter had not gauged the height of the steps. His toes slipped off the edge of the second one and down he sprawled on his face. Though he tried to protect the handkerchief by holding it up, he instinctively tried to break his fall, and the hand came down on the step and slid across the stone.

When he managed to pick himself up, he looked at the handkerchief in dismay. A good many people had been up the steps before him, and their shoes had left grime and dried mud behind them. Now the steps were cleaner, but not the handkerchief. What was worse, he saw at a glance that it was torn. "I'm sorry," he murmured and stood looking at it with his head down.

But Father Donahue was again equal to the occasion. "That's all right, me boy. That's not the first fall in the hist'ry of mankind, and it won't be the last. But ye'd best be watchin' yer feet. Both times I've seen ye, ye've been prone in the dirt." He turned and started up the steps.

Peter could not let him go like that, especially when he remembered Mrs. Morris's exclamations over the beauty and value of the handkerchief. "I'd like to say goodbye. I won't see you again, I'm afraid."

Again the father stopped. "And where are ye off to now—perhaps the North Pole?"

"No, sir, to Santa Fe."

"To Santa Fe! The saints preserve us!" Father Donahue was surprised. "Isn't that where ye were wantin' to go?"

"Yes, sir. That's where my Pa is." The words came quickly now. "Uncle Seth Bowen came from there last week and he's takin' me back with him tomorrow. Me and Brownie," he added, looking down at his pet, who was occupied at the moment with a search for a troublesome flea and had no time to do more than look up.

"That's quite a trip for a young lad like yerself. Aren't you afraid of the Indians? But I suppose," and his eyes rested on the dog, "ye'll be safe with that baist to protect ye. Well, I must go in now. Give me yer hand, and God's blessin' go with ye."

"I . . . I feel bad about the handkerchief," said Peter. "I know it must've cost a lot of money."

"Don't say anything more about it. And goodbye to ye—and to Brownie too." And the priest held out his hand.

But Peter was not satisfied. Something must be done. Suddenly an overwhelming act of atonement occurred to him. A chill ran down his spine, but he knew what he must do. With his fingers trembling, he undid the thongs by which the Pawnee scalp was fastened to his belt. By this time several ladies and gentlemen had stopped to watch, and a slight frown was appearing on the good-natured features of the priest, who was obviously anxious to be gone. Timidly Peter held out his treasure. "Won't you please take this in place of . . . ?" He could not quite finish.

Innocently the black-garbed prelate took the long black scalp lock in his hand and peered at it with curiosity. Two ladies drew closer and also looked. So did a man. To Peter's discomfiture, the latter suddenly began to laugh, but the priest did not heed him.

"What is this—some old horse's tail? Ye seem to be partial to baists." He held it nearer to his eyes for closer inspection, and one of the ladies touched it with her forefinger.

Peter was insulted. "Oh, no, sir!" he exclaimed scornfully. "It's the scalp of a Pawnee—a real one."

The lady gave a cry of horror and drew her hand back suddenly. To Father Donahue's credit he did not drop the scalp, though his hand shook visibly and he quickly lowered it from his face.

"I didn't get it myself." Peter felt he must be honest with the Church. "Uncle Seth did. He . . ."

"I couldn't think of taking it." The father held it out to the boy, his face considerably redder than it had been before.

But Peter retreated down a step. "Oh, that's all right," he said, pleased that his gift had made such an impression. "I'll get plenty of them," he added with sudden confidence. He was conscious that the people were tittering. Father Donahue too was aware of this fact, and he hastily thrust the trophy back into the boy's hand.

"No, no, you must kape it. Then ye needn't trouble about takin' any others. And now run along. Ye must have much to do, packin' up cannons and scalpin' knives. Ye needn't say anything about the handkerchief at home." He made a last move toward the door, but, feeling that he had been a bit abrupt, he stopped for the last time. "What packet will ye be sailin' on tomorrow?"

"The Queen of the Forest," answered the boy, his treasure once more safe in his grip.

Chapter Four

"Well, God bless ye, and goodbye to ye." And the plump little figure was swallowed up in the darkness within.

Peter walked home slowly. When he got there, he saw no reason for ignoring Father Donahue's advice. He said nothing about what had happened to the handkerchief.

The Queen of the Forest was to sail at nine o'clock Tuesday morning. If Peter had had his way, he would have been on the levee by six. As it was, by dint of much coaxing he was able to persuade Mrs. Morris to start a few minutes before eight. The family moved off in a little procession cheered on by several neighbor ladies who shed many tears and prophesied all sorts of dire fates for Peter. There was not one who expected ever to lay eyes on him again. But the children made up for the gloom of the grown-ups. They were openly envious and trooped along, laughing and shouting jokes and bits of advice, some serious, some facetious.

Mrs. Morris was arrayed in her best black dress and bonnet. She led the way, but was strangely silent, not uttering a word between the house and the levee. Belle walked close behind, pale and solemn as ever, clutching John by the hand; for once he was speechless. As for Eliza, she trudged along beside Peter, her eyes bigger than ever and her pigtails with their red ribbons sticking out at right angles to her head. She tried with one hand to help him with the hated carpetbag. The other was kept busy wiping away the big fat tears that rolled down her cheeks. She, too, had nothing to say, but kept biting her lips. Even Brownie seemed to sense the solemnity of the occasion, for he walked discreetly along at his master's heels, scarcely glancing to left or right or sniffing anything.

Peter himself was resplendent in his new clothes, much too resplendent for his own comfort. Uncle Seth's instructions had been decidedly sketchy, and Mrs. Morris's ideas of a suitable outfit to be worn on the plains did not agree at all with the wearer's. In fact, he had come close to rebelling several times. He was arrayed in a tight blue coat decorated with, of all things, large brass buttons. There was a gray cotton shirt under it. His long trousers, too, were gray, and his new shoes were far from comfortable. These things were bad enough, but the bag was the ultimate humiliation. He scarcely dared to think what Uncle Seth would say. The gibes of the boys on the street were, he thought, fair warning.

41

The Great Adventure Begins

He even hated to think of all the things that were packed within it. Finally, it was not only unfit for use by a boy, but it was also very heavy. His arms ached as he shifted it from one hand to the other. He was almost tempted to accept Eliza's aid, feeble though it might be, but of course he could not do that, especially with half a dozen other boys watching him and making jokes about traveling flower gardens.

At last, when his shoulders were almost dislocated, they came out from narrow Walnut Street onto the broad sunny levee. It was about as busy as it had been on Thursday afternoon and just as noisy. As Mrs. Morris had predicted, they were much too early. There was no sign of Uncle Seth or indeed of any other passengers. So she steered her party to shelter beside a huge pile of boxes and bales close by the Queen of the Forest and waited in considerable trepidation. The children, however, did not think they were too early. A visit to the levee was a rare treat for them, since they were seldom allowed there—Mrs. Morris did not know yet that Peter had been there recently—and the strange sights and sounds kept them enthralled—horses and mules, small carts and large wagons, white men and black, in all sorts of costumes, every conceivable noise from the curses of the drivers to the whinnying of the mules. And towering above all the confusion was the long line of majestic packets with their fancy woodwork and their tall slender stacks.

"Look!"

John, who was peering around the corner of a bale of hemp, pointed excitedly to the left, and the whole party turned quickly. There, marching stately one behind the other down toward the boat, came five Indians. Indians were no novelty in St. Louis, but they were usually a pretty nondescript lot and aroused little interest. Not so these five. All were tall, finely built men with long black hair hanging in straight strands in front of their shoulders. The heads of four were adorned with single feathers that stood up surprisingly straight. The fifth, who led the procession, wore a magnificent war bonnet of white eagle feathers tipped with black. It not only covered his head, but hung down his back almost to the ground. Except for the last one, who was considerably younger, all wore colored shirts tucked inside their trousers. This boy had on nothing above the waist, and Peter noticed with envy the smooth

Chapter Four

play of the muscles under the copper skin. They marched down the levee, looking straight ahead and paying no attention to the bedlam about them. Peter's flesh tingled when they mounted the gangplank to the main deck of the Queen of the Forest. For once he was glad he had the carpetbag and that Mrs. Morris had made him pack the scalp away out of sight instead of attaching it to his belt as he had planned to do. He was not at all sure they would like it. Perhaps he would not throw the satchel overboard after all.

The minutes passed, and more and more passengers arrived, for the most part men, but a few of them women leading children by the hand. Mrs. Morris noted that all but three or four were rather cheaply dressed, and she felt some pride that not one of the boys looked as "nice" as Peter. He made the same observation, but his reaction was quite different. There were several plainsmen clad in the same fashion as Uncle Seth, though none could boast so imposing a beard. But there was no sign of the hearty old-timer. As nine o'clock drew nearer and nearer, Peter became more and more worried. Where was Uncle Seth? Why didn't he come? A horrible thought struck him. Suppose he did not come at all! He had seen enough of riverfront life to know what often happened to plainsmen while on visits to civilization, and he had a chilling vision of his guardian lying drunk and unconscious in some levee saloon. He felt a little sick and had to lean back against a box.

"Oh here you are!" Peter was startled by a familiar voice and jumped to his feet. But it was not Uncle Seth, just Father Donahue standing before him, his round Irish face alight with good humor. "It's afraid I was that I was after missin' ye—that ye'd already gone aboard."

"No, sir, I can't," cried the boy. "Uncle Seth hasn't come, and it's gettin' terribly late."

"Well, he'll be here in good time, no doubt. Don't ye worry." And he introduced himself to Mrs. Morris and shook hands all around, not over-looking even Brownie. Squatting down, he scratched the little yellow head back of one ear. "Now, Brownie, mind ye've got a responsibility. Ye've got to take care of this young fighter and see that nobody gets the scalp off his head. Ye've got a pretty good scalp of yer own—at least ye would have if ye kept it clane. Perhaps it'll be more of a temptation than yer master's."

The Great Adventure Begins

Brownie accepted this doubtful compliment in silence, and the priest rose once more to his feet. "Lad," he said, looking kindly at Peter, "I'm only a poor servant of the Blessed Lord, and the likes o' me have little or nought of our own. But I'm not wantin' ye to be off across the plains without somethin' to remember me by." He thrust a pudgy hand into one pocket of his cassock. "Ye'll maybe not know just at first how to tell the time o' day by the sun and the stars; so here's an ancient watch that come from the old country over the sea." He drew forth a large silver watch with a case that snapped over its face and put it in the boy's hand. "Take it, lad, with my blessin'."

For a moment Peter stared at it unable to speak; then he looked up into the face of his friend. He had never owned a watch, scarcely even hoped to own one, at least till he was grown—he had no words to express his delight.

"Peter, thank the gentleman." Mrs. Morris was shocked by his lack of manners.

"Never ye mind, ma'am," answered the priest. "There's better thanks than words, and the light in the lad's eyes is enough." He smiled down at Peter who was exhibiting the gift to Eliza and John. "And I want ye to wear this too." He held out a small gold medal on a chain and slipped it over Peter's head. "Tuck it down under yer shirt where it won't be showin', for it's not an ornament. As long as ye wear this, the good Saint Joseph will look after ye while you look for a new home. It'll make no difference whether ye be Catholic or Protestant, and when ye say yer prayers—I'll not be surprised if ye say them oftener there than here—put in one for a poor father who'd like nothin' better than to be going with ye." He put his hand affectionately on the boy's head and then turned to Mrs. Morris. "He's a good lad, ma'am—and a first class fighter too."

Just then the Queen of the Forest emitted a thunderous blast from her whistle. They all jumped, and it so frightened Eliza that she turned pale and clutched at Peter's sleeve. Somewhere on the top deck a bell began to ring. There was a hurried rushing-about near the gangplank. Passengers crowded to the rails and began to shout goodbye to friends left ashore. Peter's terror returned with a vengeance.

"Where's Uncle Seth? Uncle Seth! Uncle Seth!" He ran frantically about looking in every direction, almost getting himself run over by a team of white horses pulling a dray. Mrs. Morris shouted commands, and Eliza wailed, but he did not hear. "Uncle Seth!"

"Now, now, now, what's goin' on here? I thought thar wuz a pack o' wolves let loose." The old plainsman's huge bulk appeared from behind a nearby wagon.

"Uncle Seth, I thought you weren't coming. I thought you were lost."

"Wal, young'un, I been in a good many tight places in my day, but I ain't been lost since I were out o' the cradle, not that I c'n remember." The blue eyes were twinkling from their hiding-place under the bushy eyebrows, but now part at least of the sparkle died out, and the man added seriously. "If ye're figgerin' on goin' out on the plains where there's Injuns and other varmints that mean ye no good, ye've got to learn to keep yer head on yer shoulders an' not go roarin' about the place like a bull-calf. That won't do no-how. Understand?"

Peter hung his head. "Yes, sir," he said. "I understand."

Uncle Seth turned to Mrs. Morris with his unfailing courtesy. "Good mornin', ma'am. I hope I see you well."

"I'm feelin' tolerable, thank you, sir." Mrs. Morris was pleased and a bit flustered. But she had sufficient presence of mind to introduce Father Donahue, who had been standing by taking in all that occurred. The two men shook hands, and the priest put in a good word for Peter as if feeling that, under the circumstances, he might need it.

"I'm sorry to have kept you waitin', ma'am," went on the plainsman, "But the feller who wuz mendin' the lock on this old gun o' mine went an' got himself drunk and didn't get the work done when he should 'av. An' I couldn't go without it." He held up the long-barreled gun he was carrying. Then he stopped and eyed Peter as if he had not noticed the youngster before. He took in his costume from head to toe. Mrs. Morris smiled with pride, but Peter's sensations were different. For a moment, the old man was silent. Then he said:

"Wal, ye look mighty elegant. Ye c'n change into yer travelin' clothes when we reach Independence. I'm afraid this outfit wouldn't last long in the saddle. Them buttons will be good fer tradin' with the Injuns, though."

This was a shock to the purchaser of the "outfit," but she dared not say

45

so. To the boy the words came as justification. He knew the suit was awful.

"Now tell yer friends goodbye and pick up yer blanket. We'd best be scramblin' aboard."

"My blanket?" Peter's face showed his consternation. "But I haven't any blanket."

"Ye ain't got a . . . !" Uncle Seth turned to Mrs. Morris. "Didn't ye get him one, ma'am?"

But she was speechless. The hideous realization that in her anxiety to have Peter "look nice" she had forgotten to provide him with his chief necessity overwhelmed her. She could only stammer, "I . . . I forgot."

Uncle Seth looked at her incredulously, and she was sure she had gone down to rock bottom in his estimation. But he was too polite to express his opinion. "Wal, ma'am, don't you worry none. We'll fit him out in Independence. They've plenty o' blankets thar, though they cost a mite more than here. An' on the boat we'll borrow one somehow."

"But there'll be one on his berth, won't there?" she asked, and saw at once that she had blundered again.

"Peter won't be sleepin' in no berth, ma'am," exclaimed the old man positively. "Them's fer old folk an' gamblers an' ladies the likes o' you. Thar's plenty o' room on the deck fer trail men." Peter was thrilled. He felt he had been restored to good standing.

Another screech from the whistle of the Queen of the Forest drowned out the conversation, and there was a flurry of bell ringing and shouting, and a general last-minute rush for the gangplank.

"Come, boy, say goodbye. Time to git aboard."

At last, the moment had come. A great lump which suddenly occupied Peter's throat prevented his obeying the instructions immediately. But he allowed Mrs. Morris, now weeping copiously, and Belle to kiss his cheek. Eliza, sobbing violently, clung to his waist, and he had to free himself gently from her clutches. His eyes were swimming, and he could not find his carpetbag until Father Donahue thrust it into his hand.

"Goodbye, Peter!" John alone maintained his equilibrium. "Bring me back a scalp!"

Suddenly there was a deafening crash of musketry over their heads, Mrs. Morris screamed and clutched her children to her. "Indians!" she

Chapter Four

cried illogically.

But Father Donahue reassured her. "That's only in the nature of a farewell salute, ma'am. The trappers and traders often fire one." He turned to look after Peter who was stumbling up the gangway. Suddenly he shouted, "Peter! Peter! Don't forget Brownie!"

The boy dropped his carpetbag and rushed back to the levee, frantically calling his pet. In a moment, with the priest's assistance, Brownie was found and caught, and carried on board just before the long gangplanks were raised into the air.

At first, Peter could not see in the darkness of the covered deck after the glare on the levee, but he quickly made out Uncle Seth's massive back and followed him through the crowd up some steps and came out on the boiler-deck above. There he squeezed into a narrow crack between two traders standing at the rail, and, clutching Brownie tightly in his arms, he stood looking down at his "family" and the city where he had lived all his life. His eyes were clear now and the lump was gone from his throat. He felt only the thrill of the beginning of an adventure.

He soon spotted Father Donohue and Mrs. Morris with her brood on the shore below. He freed one hand and waved happily. There was a great roar as the stern wheel began to turn and thrash the water into a brown spray. Slowly the levee with its crowds and its enormous piles of freight receded as the strip of dark water between it and the boat broadened. He saw Father Donahue run down to the edge of the river and, cupping his hands about his mouth, shout something to him. He leaned so perilously over the rail to hear the words that one of his neighbors caught hold of his coattails. It was hard to make out what the priest was calling, but the good father had a surprisingly big voice and soon it came booming through the uproar: "Don't let Brownie get seasick."

Peter laughed and looked at his dog; he seized one paw and waved it. The Queen of the Forest had now backed out completely from her berth between the other packets and slowly turned her blunt prow into the current. The people on the shore became smaller and smaller. The last thing Peter could make out was a little girl with two red-ribboned pigtails shaking violently in the sun and her face buried in her mother's skirts.

The Great Adventure Begins

Oregon Trail

INDEPENDENCE

Big Blue Run

LONE ELM

110 MILE CREEK

COUNCIL GROVE

SANTA FE TRAIL

Neosho River

1" = 25 miles Santa Fe Trail

Up the Missouri River from
St. Louis to Independence
and on to Council Grove

5

Up the Wide Missouri

When the Queen of the Forest headed upstream, Peter left the rail and put Brownie down on the deck. He then elbowed his way through the crowd of passengers to get to the stern for one more glimpse of St. Louis as it disappeared in the distance. But before he got there, he bumped into Uncle Seth, who found other things for him to do.

"Come on, sonny," he said, "It's time to find us a snug lay-away where we can stow our stuff and stretch out at night. Let's look us out a place up forrards if all the places ain't took already."

Peter had to search a bit before he found his carpetbag, but at last he discovered it, or rather Brownie did, near a pile of household goods. He seized it with his right hand and lugged it toward the bow, where he hoped to find his traveling companion. He did not have far to go, but there were so many men shoving and carrying all sorts of articles of furniture, boxes, and various odds and ends that he did not have an easy time getting through. Nor were the men particularly friendly. Once or twice he thought he was going to see a fight, but each time to his disappointment the angry men failed to get beyond the word stage. At last, he found a clear spot back against the outer wall of the cabin and gladly dropped his gaudy burden there. In a few minutes Uncle Seth appeared, apparently pleased that he had found such a good place.

"Wal, Peter, ye done better 'n me," he exclaimed. "I clumb up onto the hurricane deck, as they calls it, but I didn't git thar soon enough. All the places wuz took." He looked about him critically. "I reckon mebbe this is better—fer a youngster that don't carry no blanket. We're under cover here, an', if it takes a notion to rain, we won't get our skins wet. What ye got in that . . . that red and yellow contraption there?" He eyed the resplendent carpetbag with obvious disapproval.

"Oh, clothes an' things Mrs. Morris got me," Peter replied, unfastening the straps that held it shut.

"Mrs. Morris is a nice lady," observed Uncle Seth, "but it 'pears like she don't know much about outfittin' a man to cross the plains. That thar blue coat looks mighty purty, but I don't call to mind ever seein' anythin' just like it on the Trail."

"I think I'll take it off; it's gettin' kind o' hot, anyway."

"Yer Pa wouldn't know ye dressed up like that. Them buttons looks like gold dollars. Wal, we'll look about a bit in Independence an' see what we c'n fit ye out with."

Peter, who had been rummaging about in his bag with his right hand, pulled out his prized scalp. "I got this in there. Mrs. Morris wouldn't let me wear it. I thought I'd put it on when we got on the boat, but . . ." He did not finish the sentence, but glanced about to see if any of the haughty Indians were watching him.

"Why'n't ye wear it like I said?" asked Uncle Seth. "Mrs. Morris ain't here. It don't do ye no good put away under all them roses. Here, stand up. Let's tie it good so's it won't drop off in the river."

Peter did as he was told, but it was obvious that he was not enthusiastic.

"What's the matter? Don't ye like it? Ye ain't scared of it?"

"No, sir, an' I do like it, but . . ."

"But what?"

"Well, I saw some Indians come on board, an' I just thought that maybe they . . . they wouldn't like it."

Uncle Seth looked at him a moment, and then, to the boy's great embarrassment, roared with laughter. It took him several minutes to get control of himself; meanwhile Peter noticed how his large stomach rose and fell under his buckskin coat. At last, he managed to exclaim, "So ye thought ye might wake up some mornin' and find ye wuz scalped yerself! Why, Peter, ye don't know nothin' 'bout Injuns. That's the best way to make 'em respect ye. They'll think ye're a powerful smart youngster

51

to've scalped ye a man already. Anyway, them's Sioux—Brulé Sioux—an' when they see that there Pawnee topknot, they ain't goin' to have any bad feelin's. Sioux an' Pawnees don't waste no love on each other. I reckon them warriors all got some Pawnee hair of their own at home. There once wuz a Sioux warrior called 'Pawnee killer.'" He chuckled again, but he did add more seriously, "Of course, if this here wuz Sioux hair, I wouldn't exactly wave it under their noses, though they couldn't hurt ye none here."

Distinctions between the different tribes of Indians were new to Peter. He decided that it might not be a bad thing for him to pick up a little information on the subject, find out which ones were peaceful and which were not. Meanwhile, he was relieved and quickly tied the trophy to his belt.

"What are they doin' on the boat?" he asked.

"Oh," explained Uncle Seth, who had stopped laughing and now stood looking down at him, "I hear they been on to Washington t' see the President—they call him 'The Great White Father'—about some treaty or other. Could be the one they signed at Ft. Laramie in Wyoming a few years back. But settlers an' the army keep breakin' treaties and huntin' the Indians."

That question answered, Peter turned to another of greater interest. "Uncle Seth, may I look at your gun?"

"Of course, ye can," said the old man, lowering his large body to the deck and regarding his rather battered weapon with an affectionate but critical eye. He ran his fingers along the slender barrel.

"Yeh, it's a good old gun. Me an' it's been in some purty tight places together, an' it ain't failed me yet."

After a moment he held it out, and Peter examined it with awe. He, too, ran his fingers along the barrel as he had seen Uncle Seth do, and then carefully examined the stock which was surprisingly small and short in comparison. Having completed this part of his inspection, he placed the butt between his feet and, closing one eye, started to peer down into the interior with the other. Instantly, however, the gun was knocked roughly to one side.

"Didn't nobody never teach ye nothin' 'bout guns? Ye do that an' some day ye'll wake up in the Happy Huntin' Grounds with thet Pawnee. Youngster, thar's a sight o' things ye got to learn, or I won't have nothin' to show yer Pa but the spot we planted ye in. Any boy ought to have more sense than to do that. Don't ye never do that again."

Peter realized that he had done something very foolish, that he had made another bad mistake. He was both mortified and fearful that he had altogether lost the confidence of the man, with the exception of his father, whom he wanted to please the most. All he could do was murmur, "I'm sorry," and try to divert attention to other matters. He did not find that difficult to do. On one side of the barrel of the gun he had noticed a number of nicks or scratches cut into the steel with a sharp instrument. He had a strong suspicion about what they meant.

"Are these marks for the Indians you've killed?"

"What marks?" Uncle Seth pretended not to know what Peter meant.

"These," said the boy, pointing to the scratches with a dirty forefinger.

"Wal." The plainsman looked at the marks critically as if he had never seen them before. "Wal, I . . . I dunno, Peter, but I reckon they might be."

"There are nine of 'em," exclaimed Peter enthusiastically. "Nine! Have you got all the scalps? Why don't you wear 'em on your belt?" He felt he was getting back at him.

"Ye sort o' got me there. But, come to think of it, I couldn't just exactly say, except that nine'd be a purty big lot to tote around. Folks might think I wuz too big a fighter an' run away when they saw my ole carcass a-comin' around the corner."

"Uncle Seth, tell me when you got the first one. When did you kill your first Indian?"

When he had plenty of time and nothing more important to do, there were few things Seth Bowen enjoyed more than repeating the stories of his adventures. He was a good storyteller and skillful at adapting his tales to an audience that was hearing them for the first time. The various yarns were not always the same, but, generally, were accurate enough. He knew he had a most eager audience in Peter; so he leaned back against the white wall and prepared to enjoy himself.

"Wait till I light up," he said; "I can't never tell a story good unless I got a pipeful of tobacco to freshen my memory. I'm gettin' kind o' old, and my mind's so stored with all the things that've ever happened to me that I'm liable to get 'em mixed." With exasperating deliberation he proceeded to fill his pipe, pack the tobacco down in the bowl, and light up. Even then he did not start at once, but sat puffing reflectively and gazing out across the rail at the shore.

At last, just when Peter had decided that he had forgotten or changed his mind, he spoke. "I wuz tryin' to call to mind which wuz the first 'un," he apologized. "It must o' been 'bout the fall of '25, nigh on to thirty years ago, me an Tom Skerrett wuz runnin' a line of traps near the headwaters o' the Picketwire, 'bout 30 miles no'west o' Raton Mesa."

"What were you trappin'?"

"Beaver, o' course! What you s'pose?" His tone implied that the question displayed unbelievable ignorance. "We'd been back thar in the mountains 'bout two months, an' hadn't seen hide nor hair of a Injun, though we knowed thar wuz Utes in that part o' the country. We hadn't bumped into none and hadn't made any more noise than we had to. Fer a time we wuz careful 'bout where we lit our fire too, but after a while we got tired o' thet, an' sort o' lost int'rest. Got careless.

"We had purty good luck, an' wuz figgerin' on goin' into winter quarters at Taos down in the Mexican Territory. It wuz gittin' a mite cold and beginnin' to snow. Thar'd been a light fall thet night, an' I thought I'd just run up and take a last look at the trap I'd set in a crick that run into the Picketwire from the north. It wuz a fine, fresh mornin', not even any wind blowin', an' I didn't see nothin' 'cept one ole black bar huntin' a place to go to sleep in. I looked in the trap an' thar wuzn't a thing in it. Then, just when I turned, right behind a little low juniper bush, what'd ye reckon I seen?"

"I dunno—an Indian?"

"No, not a Injun himself. But one o' them had been thar not s'long before, an' he left his footprint right thar in a little patch o' snow that hadn't melted yet."

"What did you do—hide behind a tree?"

"No, sir. I cut tracks fer camp. I wasn't much bothered 'cause thar had been nobody killed by Utes fer a long time . . . they'd been on

54

their good behavior. Still, I didn't make no more noise 'n I had to, an' I didn't parade across no clearin's. I kept both eyes open an' my ears too. But I didn't see nary a thing 'cept a couple o' deer, which run out from behind some bushes.

"Between me an' camp wuz a pretty high ridge. It wuz steep and thar wuzn't much growin' on it 'cept a few spruces. I warn't particular anxious to scramble up thar an' make a good target o' myself. Thet Injun might be feelin' at peace with the world, but I know'd he'd find it agin his conscience to pass up such a good chance o' pickin' up a healthy scalp, 'specially when nobody'd ever know who done it. So I figgered I'd better look about 'n see 'f I couldn't find a better way up. I looked along thet hillside an' 'bout a quarter of a mile to the right, I sighted a sorta draw, an' made my way easy like down to it, an' started to climb up. It warn't none too easy to do it 'cause thar wuz lots o' little loose rocks an' I wuzn't aimin' to start no avalanche thet would tell all the Injuns in them mountains jest whar I wuz. So I stepped easy an' kep' my eyes peeled. But I didn't see nuthin' till I got 'bout half way up. Thet ridge wuz close to a hunderd feet high."

Here he paused, and Peter asked, as he was expected to do, "What did you see then?"

Uncle Seth indulged in two more good puffs before he resumed. "Thet same footprint. This time it wuz in the sand close to a big red rock. Thar wuz a little flat ledge thar, an' it wuz plain as it could be. I looked aroun' real careful, an' I seen thet the varmint had started to climb up in the open an' then switched over to this same gully like he didn't want to be seen neither. I didn't like thet, an' I wuz extra careful. His tracks went clean up to the top. When I got thar, I stopped ag'in, an' tuk a good squint. Thar wuz more trees on the top than on the side, a purty good growth o' spruce, but I could see between 'em an' thar warn't no sign o' thet Injun 'cept his footprints. When I got up thar, I could study 'em good an' they were new. He warn't much ahead o' me. So I wuz carefuller'n ever.

"In a few minutes I come out on the far edge an' could see down into camp. Thar wuz ole Tom acookin' breakfast. I c'd almost smell the bacon. I wuz mighty glad to see he wuz all right, but I didn't holler at

55

'im 'cause I wanted to find thet Injun. His trail turned to the right 'long the ridge, an' I wuz jest startin' to foller it when I heered a bang follered by a war whoop.

"As fer Tom, he jest nater'ly fell backwards out o' sight. I couldn't figger, though, whar he wuz a-layin'.

"But I hadn't no time to think 'bout him then. Down the hill went thet thar devil of a Ute. I seen right off thet wuz what he wuz. He wuz in a hurry to collect Tom's scalp, an' I must say it wuz a good one, 'cause he had the reddest hair I ever see an' he hadn't been near no barber fer a long time. But Mister Ute never got a chance to wear it. 'Fore he'd traveled ten yards, he wuz buryin' his nose in the sand, an' in less'n five minutes, he didn't hev' no scalp of his own to brag about."

"Did you cut it off?"

"Wal, thar warn't nobody else to do it. Anyway, it wuz mine by rights."

"But, Mr. Tom—how about him?" Peter was not yet ready to accept such situations as a matter of course.

Uncle Seth laughed. "He wuz all right. He'd jest played a good joke on thet Injun. The feller wuzn't as good a shot as he thought he wuz, an', besides, he shot from a angle, an' jest creased ole Tom's forehead 'sted o' borin' a hole in it. Tom wuz sort o' stunned an' toppled backwards into a ditch, but he weren't really hurt none. An' we didn't waste no time pullin' out o' thar 'cause thar might be some other Utes hangin' around.

"Some Injuns want to take scalps to show what great warriors they are. They like to bring 'em back to camp and celebrate, have a big dance."

Peter asked no more questions, but sat still, turning over in his mind the things he had heard and trying to understand the strange new world he was entering. It didn't fit with the Golden Rule that had been pounded into his head. Presently Uncle Seth finished his smoke, clambered to his feet, crossed to the rail, and gazed across the water.

"Look o' here," he called. "We're turnin' into the Mizzoura. Ye'd better come an' have a look."

Peter hurriedly got to his feet, and the two went together to the bow and stood staring up the broad yellow river into which the Queen of the Forest was slowly turning her blunt nose. The boy was not used to seeing open country, for he had hardly ever been out of the city. He was overwhelmed by the river and forest spreading before him—and the thought of all the new sights to come. For once he was silent as he stood beside the huge form of his friend and protector.

At its juncture with the Mississippi, the Missouri was about a mile wide and flowed slowly between low clay banks upon which grew a number of willows and an occasional cottonwood. There were no houses in sight, and Peter felt a sense of loneliness. Everything was still except for the noises of the steamer, which puffed laboriously against the current, and the raucous cawing of two crows perched on a tree. There was a small island in the center of the broad stream. It cut off part of the view, but Peter could see that a mile or so further on, the river made a bend to the left behind a high hill covered with oak trees. What was beyond that hill? What was ahead of him? Would he stay alive and reach Santa Fe and his father? As he stared at the great silent river with its tawny waves and dead trees floating by, he had a feeling that it knew the answer. He wondered what was beyond the bend—and was eager to see.

But it took the Queen of the Forest some time to reach that point, and long before then Peter's mind had turned to other things.

"When we get to Independence," he informed his companion, "I'm goin' to get me a gun like yours."

Uncle Seth turned to look at him, his eyes twinkling. "Oh, ye are, are ye?"

"Yes, sir." Secretly Peter was wondering how many nicks he would have on the barrel by this time next year.

"Go bring me mine," commanded the trapper. Peter hurried over to where it lay on the deck. Brownie, who was enjoying a nap, stretched out with his back to the wall, merely opened one eye and gazed sleepily at his master.

Peter carried the rifle carefully to Uncle Seth, who asked him if he knew how to load it. He had to confess that he did not, but was given a lesson immediately.

When the instruction was completed, Uncle Seth peered off across the water toward the little island, which they were now passing on the left.

"Sonny," he said, "thar's a big fat crow asunnin' himself on thet cottonwood. Let's see if ye can wing him?"

"Me? Now? Right here on the boat? Won't folks be surprised?" Peter

"You thought you had a gun,
not a mule, didn't you, lad?"

Chapter Five

was not anxious to make his first shot in the presence of so large an audience.

"I reckon a little surprise won't hurt 'em none. Most of 'em has heard guns go off before. Try yer hand now. Ye'll never learn younger." And he handed the boy the long, unwieldy rifle.

Peter took it in his hands, but it was so long and heavy that he could not hold it still. The barrel wobbled from side to side—he could not possibly point and take aim.

"Steady it on the rail," advised one of the men who was watching, and he helped lift it up.

But there were more difficulties. Now Peter was too tall; and he had to bend his knees to get low enough to sight at the crow, which, as the boat chugged away upstream, was rapidly being left behind.

"Best hurry up. That ole gun'll shoot a long ways, but not clean back to St. Louis."

Embarrassed and excited by the fear that his target might take wing, he tried to sight it, but he could not make the barrel stay still, and Uncle Seth made no offer to help. He pulled at the trigger. Nothing happened. It was stiff. He pulled harder—and harder. It felt as if it were cutting through his skin.

"Hurry up, boy!"

It was terrible to stand there with all these people watching him and not be able to fire. He crooked his middle finger beside the first one on the trigger and pulled for all he was worth.

Bang! There was a roar that deafened him, the gun flew up, and something hit him so hard on the shoulder that he went flying backwards and landed on the deck with his face up. He was stunned, but could hear roars of laughter from all the bystanders, and he could recognize Uncle Seth's as among the loudest.

He gathered himself together and struggled to his feet.

One man shouted, "You thought you had a gun, not a mule, didn't you, lad?"

Peter wanted desperately to rub his shoulders, but he was too proud and handed the rifle back to its owner with a laugh he had trouble in producing. "It sure can kick," he observed. "Did I hit the crow?"

"That crow didn't get hit, but I reckon he got kind o' scared, 'cause I

59

notice he moved on." Uncle Seth was watching his youthful partner closely. "Ye still figgerin' on buying a gun like this in Independence?" he asked.

"I've got to have a gun if I'm goin' to shoot bad Indians."

Again Uncle Seth gave way to his embarrassing habit of laughing aloud, the bystanders joining in with him enthusiastically. "I reckon ye do. I reckon ye do," he exclaimed after a moment. "Wal, we'll see 'bout it when we git thar."

The trip up the Missouri River occupied four days and three nights, the Queen of the Forest reaching Independence Landing about ten o'clock on Friday evening. But Peter did not find time hanging heavy on his hands. He enjoyed every minute; and, if it had not been for his eagerness to start off across the Trail, he would have been glad to have it last considerably longer. There was only one bit of excitement and even that did not last very long, but there were many things that were very interesting to a boy who had never before been five miles away from home.

First of all, he enjoyed the boat itself, with its three decks and motley crowd of travelers. It was a new experience to eat with them at the long table in the dining-saloon, where there was more food offered than he could possibly get away with—and even better than Mrs. Morris's homely fare. He never dreamed that there could be so much. Indeed there were so many plates and platters on the table that the white cloth was scarcely visible, heaps of fried chicken, rich red roasts of beef, sides of venison, many kinds of vegetables which, unlike Mrs. Morris, Uncle Seth did not make him eat, and so many different kinds of cakes and pies that he could hardly make up his mind which ones to choose. He always left the table wishing he had not been quite so greedy, but, when he returned for the next meal, he forgot his good intentions and ate just as much as before. Brownie also got more than he needed.

It was fun to sleep out on deck. He was glad he did not have to be shut up in a cabin, but could stretch out with Brownie at his feet where it was cool. He could see everything that was going on and hear the thrilling stories told by the trail men, some of them so thrilling that they raised gooseflesh all over his body. He also liked to watch the lonely lights in the farmhouses on the distant shore as they seemed to slide along noiselessly under the railing and to listen to the steady puffing of the engine and the splashing of the water thrown up by the great stern wheel.

He listened intently to many tales of steamboat explosions and of wrecks caused by the vicious snags for which both the Missouri and the Mississippi were notorious. He had no desire to be involved in one of the former, but the only drawback to hitting a snag would be a delay in reaching Independence. He was taken below deck and shown the snag-chamber, a watertight compartment, which would, it was hoped, be the only portion of the hull pierced should an accident occur and so would keep the boat from going to the bottom at once.

At first, he was not exactly certain what a snag was and how it did its damage, but it was not long before he had a chance to see for himself. This was the one real excitement of the voyage.

On the afternoon of the second day out, not long before they came to the little town of Boonville, there was a shout that a boat was coming. Peter, with Brownie by him as usual, hurried to the bow to see it. He found himself a few minutes later standing next to the rail beside two of the Sioux chiefs. He was just a trifle uncomfortable, especially when he saw one of them stare intently at the scalp hanging at his belt. He was even more uncomfortable when with a grunt and a gesture he pointed it out to the attention of the other, the one who had worn the spectacular war bonnet when they came aboard. They both peered at it with keen interest and exchanged several remarks in their guttural language. Peter felt himself turning all colors, especially red and white, and he fervently wished they had chosen some other place from which to watch the approaching packet.

To his great relief, however, he was soon joined by Uncle Seth, who, taking in the situation at a glance, engaged the two Indians in a conversation, chiefly by means of signs and a few unclear words. Peter saw that they were listening eagerly and that they both covered their mouths with their hands and stared at him in a way that made his blood run cold. Then, in turn, they reached out and, taking the scalp between their fingers, examined it with the utmost care, and then exchanged ominous looks.

After they had satisfied their curiosity, the older one placed his hand

61

on Peter's head. He felt himself being scalped on the spot. "Fine boy—big brave . . . come live in my lodge."

Peter felt some relief, though the thought flashed through his mind that perhaps he would have no choice. Nevertheless, he managed to answer:

"I can't. I'm goin' to see my father."

The chief evidently did not understand, for he turned to Uncle Seth, who shook his head and, pointing toward the southwest, said, "Santa Fe." Whereupon the chiefs again concentrated on the approaching boat.

The latter was now coming close and greeted the Queen of the Forest with a long blast on its whistle. It was answered with another long blast.

"The William Clark, that's who she is!" exclaimed one of the passengers who had been trying to make out her identity. "I know her by the way her . . ."

But he did not finish his sentence.

Suddenly the William Clark stopped short and so violently that the tall slender stacks swayed forward and then backward as if they would snap off at their bases. Boxes and barrels crashed down from their piles with such a noise that it carried across the water to the startled spectators on the Queen of the Forest.

"Hit a snag, by gum!" cried the man standing on Peter's left.

There was great excitement on board the William Clark. Peter could see people rushing about. There was a great ringing of bells and belching out of clouds of white steam as one shrill whistle followed another. There was also excitement on the Queen of the Forest, much bell ringing and shouting of orders. She slowed down until only enough power was maintained to keep her from being pushed downstream by the current.

The crowd at the bow became so large that one of the officers hurried forward and ordered many of the people to go back toward the stern before the boat plunged its over-weighted prow down into the muddy river. Peter was standing close to the rail and was one of those allowed to stay. As he watched, he could see that the wounded packet was listing to the left. He could also see a man on the bow lowering a long line into the water and shouting figures to an officer leaning over the railing on the upper deck. He knew enough to understand that he was taking soundings to find out how deep the river was.

"The river ain't much more'n waist deep yonder," observed the man who had first recognized the William Clark. "There ain't no danger of her sinkin'. If she's hit bad, she'll jes' settle down in the mud an' set there till they pull her out."

Sure enough, in a very little while the boat ceased to settle and remained stuck at an angle. She looked so funny that Peter laughed. Then he pictured the dining-saloon with all the furniture and plates in a heap along one wall, and he wondered if there had been much of that good food on the tables. In a few minutes, a small boat put out from the Queen of the Forest with the first mate sitting in the stern and two deckhands pulling at the oars. They rowed over to the wreck, and the officer climbed aboard. Before long they returned with word that no help was needed for the moment, but that the captain asked that some of his passengers be carried back to Boonville. The rowboat made two more trips to the William Clark, returning each time with three strangers, and in a short while the Queen of the Forest was once more puffing away up the river.

"What's a snag like?" Peter asked Uncle Seth as they made their way to the stern for a last look at the crippled vessel. Having seen one in action, he wanted to know more. Their own boat was following the channel toward the south bank of the river and was hurling great chocolate-colored waves against the shore, which at this point was a steep clay bank rising from the water. However, just as the old man was about to embark upon an explanation of snags and their ways, he was interrupted by the boy.

"Look at that tree!" he cried, pointing to a large, half-dead cottonwood that stood on the edge of the bank, its scraggly branches silhouetted against the clear blue of the sky. As they watched, a great wave from the wake of the boat pounded the bank, which then crumbled away. The old tree shuddered, tossed its half-naked branches frantically upward, and fell with a tremendous splash into the river and was borne swiftly downstream.

Uncle Seth pointed a stubby finger after it. "See them roots," he asked, "stickin' out where they was broke off?"

"Yes, sir," said Peter.

"Wal, thar's yer snags. Purty soon that ole tree's liable to git stuck in the mud. After awhile it'll git waterlogged and sink out o' sight, but them roots'll stick up and mebbe a boat'll come along and git its bottom stove full o' holes like the William Clark. Understand, sonny?"

Peter did understand and let the matter drop. He had another question to ask; yet it was one he had some trouble putting into words. It was not until he had settled down again in his corner with Uncle Seth and Brownie that he finally asked it.

"Uncle Seth, what—what did you tell those Indians about me?"

The old man looked a bit guilty. He pulled a plug of tobacco from his pocket, bit off a mouthful, and stared at the deck a few feet from the railing. But Peter saw that he was watching him out of the corner of his eye.

"What did you tell 'em?" he demanded.

"Oh, nuthin' much, I reckon."

"Yes, you did, too. C'm on an' tell me." Peter had by now lost most of his awe of his companion, and, furthermore, he knew he was being teased. So he persisted. "What did you say?"

"Wal," Uncle Seth turned and gazed reflectively at Brownie, who was lying with his nose between his paws, his big brown eyes watching every movement his friends made. "Wal, I jes' tole 'em not to be figgerin' none on eatin' that pup thar."

"On eating Brownie!" Peter gasped.

"Sure 'nough. Thar's nuthin' a Sioux likes better'n a good fat dog. Serve 'em at all their feasts. An' Brownie don't look like he'd been on starvation rations. Fact is, he'd make a purty good dinner." And he gave the dog a dig with his shoe.

Peter hastily put out a protecting hand, and all that remained of Brownie's tail moved slowly from side to side. "Nobody's goin' to eat him!" This was something new, an unheard of danger that had never occurred to him.

"I tole 'em they'd better leave him alone, 'cause you wuz a powerful fighter. I tole 'em jes' how you killed thet Pawnee single-handed, an' said you had three more scalps like it hangin' in yer lodge. I said you wuz a dangerous shot with a rifle, an' you had a temper like a grizzly bar."

Peter did not know whether to be pleased or not. Remembering his adventure with the crow, he knew he was being teased again. But by this time he realized that he was in for his full share of teasing, and, anyway, if Brownie was safer, he was satisfied. So he said nothing more, but sat pulling one of his pet's silky ears and winding the little white topknot about his forefinger.

The rest of the trip was uneventful. They stopped at Boonville to take on a few more passengers and drop off those from the stranded William Clark, but the stop was not long, and few people went ashore. Peter and Uncle Seth watched. "A while back some folks started on the trail here. A few still do." There were no more stops except the routine ones to pick up wood for the engines, and late Friday night the Queen of the Forest pulled near the dimly lighted wooden pier at Independence Landing.

The first stage of the long trip was about to end.

6

Peter Gets a New Outfit

It was very dark. There was no moon, and the only light came from the feeble lanterns swinging from the hands of the few men on the landing. So Peter could not make out anything that lay beyond, whether houses or trees. But there was plenty of noise. Shouts from the men and the great roar of the water churned up by the stern wheel reverberated from the blackness. The Queen of the Forest was slowly pulled up to the wharf, where the waiting men lashed it with heavy ropes to thick stakes that had been driven deep into the ground. The strain caused the timbers of the boat to creak, but all held firm. In a few moments the passengers poured down the gangplank and disappeared into the all-enveloping darkness.

Peter and Uncle Seth, having little to carry, were among the first ashore. Peter made sure that Brownie was at his heels, for he feared that, if he lost sight of him even for a second, he might vanish in the confusion and darkness. The hill up from the river was steep, and the carpetbag was no lighter than it had been on the levee in St. Louis, but Peter understood that he was expected to put up with hardships and asked for no help. He suspected that Uncle Seth was aware of his difficulties, but, if he were, the old trapper said nothing and did not offer to carry it.

When they reached level ground, they made their way among sheds and cabins, which Peter could just make out in the darkness. He could hear voices all about him, and once or twice they bumped into almost invisible men, but neither he nor Uncle Seth spoke. It was, he thought, the darkest night he had ever encountered. Unfortunately, it was not too dark for the mosquitoes to be about their business, and the fact that his hands were not free gave them an unusual advantage. In a short while, the settlement was left behind. At least, he could not make out any more houses, and the babble of voices subsided. He could tell they were following a road by feeling the ruts with his feet. But in a few minutes, Uncle Seth turned off to the right and struck off across country. Peter could barely see the large body ahead of him and followed in silence.

After they had stumbled along for a few minutes, Uncle Seth called back over his shoulder, "Thar ain't no use o' spendin' good money fer a bed in a boardin'-house. Ye'll have to git used to sleepin' out, and ye might's well begin tonight. It'll be quieter, anyway."

Peter managed to find breath enough to say that was fine and that he would rather camp out. But he was not at all sure that he had been heard. He could not possibly tell how long they walked, but it seemed to be forever. At last, after he had shifted the bag from one hand to the other so many times that he expected his arms to be pulled bodily from their sockets, Uncle Seth came to a halt beneath a large tree.

"Here's our campsite," he said, apparently not in the least out of breath. "Drop thet bag o' your'n an' settle down fer a good nap. It's s'warm, ye won't need a blanket over ye, and ye can lie on a corner o' mine."

It was warm, even hot, and the boy was glad to be without any covers. He did not care even to have the blanket under him, but he did not want to reject his friend's offer, so he lay down as directed with Brownie close by his side.

He did not have as good a sleep as he was expected to have. This was the first time he had ever spent the night outdoors, except on the boat, and he was too excited to settle down. Moreover, he was unable to get comfortable. Squirm as he might, he could not escape a sharp-pointed little rock that insisted on digging into his back. He would have liked to crawl away from Uncle Seth and find a soft spot, but at first he thought it best to stay where he was.

Uncle Seth obviously experienced none of his comrade's difficulties. He had no sooner stretched out than he was sound asleep. There was no room for doubt, for Uncle Seth was not a silent sleeper. Peter had heard snores before—Mr. Morris's breathing had been audible at quite a distance. But he had never heard anything like the sounds which came with perfect regularity from the sleeping form beside him. The old man had lain down flat on his back, and when the moon rose, his companion could see the vast stomach rising and falling peacefully. He listened fascinated. A long, sucking sound accompanied each upward motion of the abdomen, to be followed in a moment by a blast that almost frightened the boy and must have blown any lurking mosquitoes yards away. He noticed that a katydid which had been chanting mournfully when they lay down, became silent, and he wondered if it had been scared off. He wondered, too, if Uncle Seth snored like that on the plains and, if he did, why the Indians had not found and scalped him as he slept. At last, deciding that the concert was scheduled to continue till morning, he rolled off the blanket and found a soft, grassy little hollow between two large roots. Sleep finally overcame his excitement.

When he awoke, it was bright daylight, and Uncle Seth was sitting on his blanket having a peaceful smoke, while Brownie made the tour of inspection he had not been allowed to make the night before.

Peter sat up and rubbed his eyes.

"Ye shore slep' well, sonny," said Uncle Seth, "jes' like ye was used to it."

Peter agreed politely. He was tempted to ask for an explanation of the snoring problem, but decided to postpone that for the time being and contented himself with a silent inspection of the offending nose. He could not figure out how such a small one could produce such an enormous volume of sound. The examination was interrupted shortly by the owner of the nose, who declared that a little breakfast would sit well with him, and that, if Peter had no objections, they would go off and look for some.

Naturally, there were none, and the trio was soon striding off cross-country toward Independence nearly two miles away. This walk resembled the one of the night before, except that there was plenty of light and it was longer. The carpetbag was just as heavy, and Peter's arms were already sore, but nothing was said and no halts were made until they reached Court House Square in Independence, where Uncle Seth encountered a friend and stopped "to swap a few lies."

Peter was really not interested in architecture; so he looked at the people moving about. He did observe that the tall, narrow Court House was not much like the squat, gray unfinished one at home. There was, however, plenty to watch in the Square, and he missed nothing. Independence, as the eastern end of both the Santa Fe and Oregon Trails, was one of the busiest towns of its size in the country. All of this activity centered in the square with its rows of stores and boarding houses. Dozens of huge covered wagons like the one Peter had seen rushed onto the boat that afternoon on the levee in St. Louis were drawn up around the Court House. It all seemed so long ago that he was startled when he realized that it hadn't been ten days. He wondered if his acquaintance from the levee might still be in Independence. How startled he would be if they met! But Peter did not see a familiar face among all the crowds of people who were milling about in the streets, climbing in and out of the wagons, and yelling vociferously at each other. He was surprised at the number of women, children, and dogs, and feared that Brownie might become involved in serious fights before they started on the Trail. He noticed that oxen were hitched to some of the wagons instead of horses or mules; they all looked tired and sleepy, and he thought how exhausted they would be when they reached the end of their long trips.

In a few minutes Uncle Seth finished his conversation and called to Peter to come and get breakfast. He led the way and soon turned into the front door of a house at the far end of the Square. Peter was not at all sure that dogs were welcome inside, but he made up his mind to say nothing unless he or Brownie was spoken to, and in they all went. There was a long table in the middle of the room, each side lined with rough looking men busily engaged in talking and disposing of quantities of food and coffee. The air was thick with tobacco smoke and the tempting odor of frying bacon. Through a door at one end of the room, waitresses came and went, their arms full of dishes, somehow or other managing to avoid disastrous collisions.

69

Uncle Seth eyed the table carefully, but there were no empty places; so there was nothing to do but wait, standing with their backs to the wall. Looking out a window, Peter could see a number of men washing their faces and hands at basins placed in a row on a bench just outside. He looked at his own hands and even he realized that they needed a long session with soap and water. He was, in fact, actually on the point of slipping out and making the needed repairs, when two men pushed their chairs back from the table and left them vacant. So the soap was allowed to wait.

"Sit down, an' fill up," Uncle Seth said with a gesture toward the chairs. "Brownie, you git in thar under the table and mebbe a few scraps may jes' happen to fall on the floor."

The dog understood his instructions and crawled in between his master's legs. There was no giving or taking of orders for food. They had scarcely seated themselves and Peter had barely had time to discover that at previous meals, eggs and tomatoes had been served, when a large red-haired waitress deposited two heavy china plates and two cups of steaming coffee in front of them, and then reached over with a brawny arm and shoved a plate of large brown biscuits in their direction.

"Bacon up in a minute," she shouted over her shoulder as she left.

Peter had not yet learned to drink coffee. He was used to milk, and had had it on the Queen of the Forest, but he saw none here, and silently munched away on the biscuit, which tasted rather good, although it was heavy and dry. The bacon, when it came, was very salty, and he looked about desperately for some water, but there was none in sight. So he gave up, and, taking advantage of the fact that everybody was occupied and the red-haired waitress off in the kitchen, he quietly slipped a slice of bacon from the platter to his plate and then to the floor under the table.

He felt Brownie rub against his leg as he went after the tidbit. Then, suddenly, from under the table came a fearful uproar—snarls, growls, yelps, every sort of sound made by a dog in anger, by a dozen dogs, it seemed to Peter. There was, moreover, a wild scuffling. His legs were bumped into by some animal, and he drew them back without thinking. He jumped down from his chair and peered into the darkness. All he could see was a confused mass of hair—a tan and white blur.

"Brownie! Brownie!" he shouted and tried to reach in for his pet. But he could find nothing to catch hold of, and the battle continued.

Uncle Seth joined him, reaching in with his big, knotted hands. So did a burly, black-bearded man who had been sitting across the table. Squatting on his haunches, he thrust a huge hairy arm into the melee, and, catching the white dog by a hind leg, began to pull.

"Haul out yer dog," he commanded, and Uncle Seth caught hold of some part of Brownie and jerked. But the fighters had too tight a hold on each other and refused to let go. Suddenly, Peter felt himself pushed to one side and looked up to see the big waitress throwing a pitcher of water upon the combatants.

"Now, pull!" she ordered.

Reaching in, he managed to catch hold of a tan leg. He and Uncle Seth, obeying orders from above, pulled together, and in a second Brownie was out, somewhat bloody, but not seriously damaged. Peter caught him up in his arms. By the time he had gotten to his feet, the waitress was removing an empty plate from the table as if nothing out of the ordinary had occurred. As for the big man opposite, he contented himself with kicking the white dog, a kind of setter, off into a corner and resumed his attack upon a pile of pancakes. To Peter's amazement, nobody else appeared to have paid any attention. But he had had enough. Telling Uncle Seth that he would wait outside, he carried his pet out to the washbasins, where he went through the motions of washing blood and dirt from his hands. While he was about this task, a good-natured cook in a soiled apron appeared at a window and threw a piece of raw meat in their general direction.

"Heah's somethin' foh yo' houn'," he drawled. "'Tain't so fresh, but ah reckon he ain't proud."

"Thank you," said Peter. Brownie downed his breakfast in two gulps.

Uncle Seth emerged from the house in a few minutes. Seeing the row of basins reminded him of a duty not done; so he proceeded to wash his face and hands thoroughly—and then asked Peter if he had done so. For once in his life Peter was glad to be able to say yes. Unlike Mrs. Morris, Uncle Seth accepted this statement and didn't bother to make an inspection. After all, the boy was old enough to know that he ought to keep himself as clean as circumstances permitted. Perhaps nothing else that had happened made him feel quite so grown-up, and after that he was much more careful about his appearance than he had ever been when under constant orders to "wash behind your ears."

"Wal, Peter,"—Uncle Seth began half his conversations with the boy in the same way—"Wal, Peter, the next thing fer us to do, I reckon, is to try and scare you up a hoss an' a blanket an' some clothes that'll do ye some good."

"Yes, sir."

"We'll go 'cross the Square an' see what ole Jack Franklin has in the shape o' shirts an' blankets. Then we'll try to pick up some hoss-flesh. Thar ought to be somethin' ye can ride in one o' them emigrant camps. Come along. We ain't got time to waste."

"Will we start out on the Trail as soon as we get them?"

"Jest about. A feller I saw in the boardin'-house said my pardner's pushed ahead with his wagon, and left word he'd wait fer me at Council Grove." This piece of news gave Peter a start. They were walking rapidly across the Square, dodging horsemen and an occasional wagon-team.

"Aleck Cochran—him and me's worked together off an' on fer ten years now. He's got a wagon haulin' freight to Santa Fe to sell in Spiegelberg's store where your Pa works, an' I goes along to help him keep the Injuns from helpin' themselves to it."

"Is Council Grove far from here?"

"'Bout a hunderd an' fifty mile. We'd orter make it by Tuesday."

By this time, they were in front of a large store across the front of which was a large sign with peeling paint that said, "Owens and Aull, Merchants." It was hard to read, because Samuel Owens had been killed in Mexico six years earlier. The store continued with new owners. Uncle Seth went in, and Peter and Brownie followed. Peter never enjoyed a shopping expedition, particularly one for the purpose of buying clothes for him, but this one was as painless as it could possibly be. In the first place, the clothing to be purchased was not of the city variety, and in the second Uncle Seth was, at least as far as Peter's limited experience went, no ordinary shopper. He knew just what he wanted and wasted no time going after it or lingering to discuss fine points. He was not, on the other hand, a careless buyer. When the ordeal was over, Peter emerged from the store with two good shirts made of deerskin, a stout pair of trousers of the same material, a pair of boots that would certainly keep out the wet and cold, and two warm woolen blankets. The subject of a gun was not raised by either Uncle Seth or Peter. The hated carpetbag and its contents were abandoned to their fate, but not before the brass buttons had been cut from the blue coat. Peter remembered what Uncle

Seth had said about trading them to Indians and slipped them into a pocket of his new pants.

The next thing was the acquisition of a good pony. He had not yet confessed that he had not once in his life been astride a horse of any sort or description, for it was an admission he dreaded to think about. He was very eager to ride and had no doubt that he could do so. Yet he did have his doubts about the first attempt, and his excited anticipation about the actual purchase was somewhat dampened by these secret fears. However, he said nothing, and silently accompanied Uncle Seth and Brownie to the place where his future mount was supposed to be waiting.

They did not have far to go. When they had walked a short distance out of town, he spied, under a grove of oak trees to the right of the road, a collection of covered wagons, near which stood a number of oxen chewing their cuds in a melancholy manner. On close inspection, he noticed that these beasts were not so fat and sleek as the ones he had seen in the Square. Rather, they were very thin and their ribs very much in evidence.

Uncle Seth had friends everywhere, and it was not long before he encountered one leaning against the frame of one of the wagons. The man, whom Uncle Seth addressed as "Rube," had only one eye and sometime during his life had lost most of his teeth. In contrast to Uncle Seth, he was far from clean, and Peter observed that he failed to handle his tobacco juice with the dexterity and precision displayed by the latter.

Uncle Seth opened the conversation. "Wal, Rube, what sort of a trip d'ye have?"

"Fair to middlin'," was the reply. The speaker aimed a stream of brown liquid at a puddle—and missed.

"How long'd it take ye?"

"'Bout two months, I reckon. I didn't take notice, 'specially."

"Which way'd ye come?" The brief answers failed to discourage Uncle Seth. "By Bent's Fort or the dry way?"

"Dry," replied Rube, squatting on the ground and making another attempt at the puddle to the utter ruination of an unfortunate dandelion.

"How's the Comanches?"

"Didn't see none. Heerd they was about, though!"

After this there was a pause broken only by the sound of Rube's spitting.

73

Then Uncle Seth: "Anybody hereabouts got a pony he'd like to sell—somethin' this younker c'n ride back along the Trail?"

For a moment there was no answer, then: "Hank Peters got a sorrel. He mought sell it. Dunno."

"Wal, Peter, let's go have a try. Hank knows hoss-flesh. Anythin' he has'll be good. 'Bye, Rube."

"'Bye." Rube neither altered his position nor looked up, but instead tried another shot at the puddle, scoring another miss, but giving a very startled grasshopper a dose—rather, a bath—of his own medicine, which sent him flying off with an indignant whirr.

"Sort o' shiffless," remarked the old man as they walked off. "Dunno why he warn't scalped long ago."

In a few minutes Hank Peters was located and the question of a horse broached. Yes, he had a sorrel pony he had bought in Santa Fe. Yes, he would sell it, if he was offered enough for it. Hank was very different from Rube, a big, clean-shaven man with quantities of blonde hair and sunburned cheeks. He led the way through the camp to a place where horses were tethered and then picked out a small brown one with a white foot and a white star on its forehead. Uncle Seth examined it with the greatest care, missing no point or feature—eyes, back, teeth, and hoofs—all came in for close inspection.

"Looks purty good," he reported when he had finished.

"Not so bad," said Hank. "Name's Pluto. Dunno why."

"Got a saddle fer him? The younker ain't got any."

Hank did not reply, but disappeared into one of the wagons, emerging a moment later with a very magnificent saddle adorned with all sorts of silver trimmings.

"Hmm, Mexican," observed Uncle Seth. "'Fraid that's too fine fer Peter here. His Pa ain't got money to waste."

Hank turned a critical eye on Peter, and the boy felt for a moment that he would like to change places with the pony. "Whose is he?" he finally asked.

"Abel Blair's. Know him?"

The man's interest plainly increased. "Oh! Abel's!" he exclaimed. "Know'd he had one back in the settlements. What's he doin' here?"

Chapter Six

"Goin' to find Abel. Had his mind set on it, an' he bedeviled this ole fool into takin' him."

"'Fraid Peter ain't a smart enough horseman to set in that saddle," he remarked, eyeing a stirrup.

"Shore he is," scoffed Hank. "You say he's Abel's boy. I never seen Abel thrown yet, even if he does stand behind a counter all day. Come on, sonny, let's see you mount."

Now came the test. Peter was not sure just what to do first, but he was determined not to let that stop him. Stepping to one side of Pluto, he seized the saddle and started to raise one foot into the stirrup.

"Hey there! What'r you doin'?' demanded Hank excitedly.

Peter thought it was obvious that he was getting on the pony.

"Don't you know no better'n to try to get on a hoss's right side?"

Peter did not know, but he just said, "I forgot," and scurried around to the left side.

Raising his body to the saddle was no easy feat, and neither man offered to help or advise him, but merely stood off and watched. Finally, fixing the toes of his foot in the wide stirrup, he gripped the leather side of the saddle, since he could not reach the pommel, and with great effort succeeded in reaching his destination. Pluto was not a large pony, but the ground seemed a long way off.

Hank now adjusted the stirrups so that Peter could stand up in them comfortably, and also ordered him to take the reins in his left hand. "Now then, let's see what sort of a rider you are." Peter heard a sharp slap administered to Pluto's rear, and they were off.

Pluto did not run. He just trotted. But trotting is always a painful experience for a beginner—and everything was new to Peter. He had never in his whole life been so bumped. He thought his backbone would be rammed out through the top of his head. It did not take half a minute for both feet to lose all contact with the stirrups—he kept his seat only by clinging desperately to the saddle-horn. The horse evidently had reasons for wanting to go somewhere—and he knew very well just where that somewhere was. He headed for that place, dodging in and out of trees that were much too close together and under branches that were much too close to the ground. In a moment Peter's hat was knocked off.

Peter Gets a New Outfit

He tried to hold his feet tight against Pluto's ribs, but they would not stay there and banged about like the abandoned stirrups. And the jolting just got worse. Yet through it all he hung on.

Bump! Bump! Up and down! He saw a large tree directly in their path and shut his eyes. He was flung to one side as Pluto swerved. He bent low to avoid an overhanging limb.

Suddenly, it was all over. The horse stopped short. A pale and badly shaken boy sat on his back. But still on his back, not flat on the earth.

Uncle Seth and Hank came running up.

"Why'n't you rein him in?" called the latter, seizing the bridle. Peter had no breath to answer. "Why'n't you keep yer feet in the stirrups?"

Now the boy found breath enough to answer indignantly, "They wouldn't stay!"

"Ain't you never rode a hoss before?" the man demanded as Uncle Seth lifted his charge to the ground.

"No, sir."

Uncle Seth looked at him. "Wuz that yer first ride?"

"I never had a chance before." And he leaned against a convenient stump.

"Wal, ye stayed on," his friend observed. "Reckon ye can learn. An' we'll take the saddle too."

Hank grinned. "That saddle's his'n already. He can use it till he's good enough to ride bareback like the Injun boys. Jes' pay me fer the pony an' fergit the trappin's."

Uncle Seth drew the familiar cotton bag from some secret place on his person and counted out the money, how much Peter did not see.

"Say h'lo to Abel when you see him," said Hank as they left.

And off they walked, four now where they had been three, Uncle Seth in the lead, Peter and Pluto, and Brownie bringing up the rear.

Chapter Six

7

Starting Out on the Trail

They went back to town to pick up Uncle Seth's horses and pack up the few supplies he had bought that morning. When he took the Prairie Rose to St. Louis, Uncle Seth had left the horses in the care of a friend who lived in Independence. It did not take long to reach the house and put the bridles and saddles on the animals. The friend was away on a trip to Fort Leavenworth; so there was no temptation to linger and "trade lies." The little party was soon back at the former Owens and Aull store, where they collected their purchases and had a hurried lunch of bread and jelly. Only the packing remained to be done.

Uncle Seth's saddle horse was a large black mare called "Bonita." This name mystified Peter, who was not familiar with Spanish and who wondered, therefore, if the old man had somehow acquired an equine phenomenon who subsisted on a diet of bones. But Uncle Seth soon explained that the name meant "beautiful" and had been attached to the mare when he had bought her from a Mexican trader in Santa Fe. Now, Bonita had passed the bloom of her youth, and Peter thought, without saying so, that the name no longer fit.

But it was the packhorse that was the center of attention. He was a solid looking animal with a bad left eye. His owner maintained that this infirmity, far from being a disadvantage, was really a blessing, for it kept Blanky—he too was of Mexican birth, and his original name had been Blanco in honor of his color—from seeing the loads that were being hoisted onto his back.

As he watched the loading process, Peter understood what Uncle

Seth meant and wondered how one horse could carry so much without caving in. Blankets, clothing, and quantities of food were packed on with a skill that baffled the boy now, but that soon enough he would try to achieve. He was really shocked at what seemed to be the brutal way in which the packsaddle was fastened in its place. The old trader pulled the straps under Blanky's stomach as tight as he could and then, placing one large, moccasined foot against the animal's ribs, threw all his strength and weight into tightening the cinch still more to the accompaniment of heart-rending groans from his victim.

"Don't that hurt him?" Peter finally asked, unable to stand the performance any longer.

Uncle Seth gave another mighty pull and then restored his right foot to the earth.

"Naw," he answered contemptuously. "That don't hurt him none. He's jes' play-actin'. He sucks in a lot o' air and blows out his belly as big as he can. Watch him now, an' he'll let go, and these tarnation girths'll be plenty loose. I never seen a hoss yet that couldn't look after hisself. Don't waste yer sympathy."

Peter did watch and, sure enough, although he could detect no deflation of Blanky's abdomen, a little cautious experimentation with his finger soon showed that the strap was far from painfully tight—nor did Blanky reveal the slightest evidence of discomfort from then on.

The packing did not consume a great deal of time, and in a little while Uncle Seth called to Peter to "git on." Peter had a real problem— what to do about Brownie? Could the little dog run fast enough and could he hold out? Perhaps he had better try to persuade him to ride on the saddle in front of him. But he was not at home there himself and decided to wait and watch what happened. After all, Brownie did run about a lot at home.

So once more he climbed upon his precarious perch. At last, the time had arrived. To Peter it was a great moment, the greatest in his life, but no one else appeared to be in the least excited. Two old cronies of Uncle Seth's watched from the shade of a nearby tree, shouting advice and witticisms between shots of tobacco juice. He and Uncle Seth might be starting off for the other end of town for all the notice they attracted. It was all part of the day's work. But Peter secretly wished that Father Donahue and some of the boys from home could have been on hand to see him. And maybe Eliza. He could imagine how big her eyes would be and how her pigtails would shake.

Then Uncle Seth cried, "All right, let's git goin'!" He dug his heels into Bonita's flanks and clucked to her in a way that Peter tried in vain to copy.

Uncle Seth went first, slouched over in his great Mexican saddle, his short fat legs looking shorter than ever as they dangled at the mare's sides, his broad red beard spread protectively over his chest. He held a strong rope that led Blanky, who seemed to be walking in his sleep. Last of all came Peter in his uneasy seat, looking anxiously down at Brownie, who trotted beside him just as if he had done it every day of his life.

It did not take long to leave Independence behind, and soon they were jogging along a country road. Secretly Peter felt a little disappointed. He was not sure just what he had expected, but this was an ordinary road with farmhouses and cornfields on each side. Yet even this was new to him. He had spent his whole life in a city and had never really seen anything else until the trip up the Missouri with Uncle Seth. He had not suspected that there were so many flowers in the world, or trees either, for that matter. He did not know the names any of them, but without realizing it, he responded to their beauty. He kept his eyes wide open to take in the unfamiliar scene. Meanwhile Brownie found all sorts of fascinating things in the tall grass beside the road and ran about, sniffing the ground as he went. So far as he was concerned, this was a dog's heaven.

By early afternoon, however, his master was not aware of flowers, trees, or anything else—other than his own aches and pains. He had been up since dawn, had walked miles, and ridden a horse for the first time in his life. He was tired. In fact, he could not remember when he had ever been so tired—or so sore. His knees hurt, and other parts of his anatomy were protesting against the unusual punishment to which they were being subjected. He was convinced that there was no skin left at the base of his spine.

To his great relief, when they came to a rather large stream, Uncle

Seth, speaking for the first time since they left the Square, exclaimed, "Here's the Big Blue Run. When we git acrost, we'll git down an' stretch our legs a bit."

The Big Blue was not deep and was forded without difficulty. As soon as he reached dry land, he pulled Bonita to a halt and dismounted. He did so with ease and agility, but not so poor Peter. When he took his feet out of the stirrups and tried to straighten out his legs, the pain in his knees almost made him cry out. But he bit his lip and tried his best to climb down and walk about as if nothing at all were the matter. Uncle Seth said nothing, but, as so often happened, Peter was aware that he was watching out of the corner of his eye. The old man came over and, taking the reins from the pommel of Pluto's saddle, drew them over the pony's head and let them hang.

"Always let yer reins hang like that, sonny. A good hoss won't never run away when his reins is hanging—unless he's stampeded—or close to home."

Peter walked about stiffly for a few minutes and then sank down on a rock, and Brownie, apparently not in the least tired, sat down beside him, licking Peter's grimy hands with his little pink tongue. For the first time Peter was homesick. The only other time in his life that he had felt like this was when his father had gone away and left him with the Morrises. But then he was just lonely for "Pa." Now there was a big lump in his throat, and he wanted desperately to cry. The impulse filled him with shame and fury. What would Uncle Seth say? So he gritted his teeth and sat still, twisting Brownie's bedraggled topknot about his forefinger.

Uncle Seth paid no attention to him, but after inspecting the saddle girths, suddenly turned his attention to his surroundings. "Wal, I reckon," he remarked after a moment, not addressing Peter any more than the horses, "this is a purty good place to camp. Thar's water an' wood. An' it's gittin' kind o' late. We've come 'bout twenty mile. Peter, you hustle yerself 'roun' an' see if ye can't find some wood while I unpack."

Peter would have preferred to stay where he was, but orders were orders, and he soon discovered that he felt better working than sitting still. In a short time Uncle Seth had the packs and saddles off the horses, which he tethered to some small trees, remarking that they were too near home to be turned loose. The ropes were long, and there was plenty of grass within their reach.

Having finished these chores, he directed his attention to building a fire, showing Peter just how he did it, and then frying a slab of ham. Silent as he had been in the saddle, he now kept up a running conversation and saw to it that his companion had no idle moments. He had him make toast, bring in more wood, and attend to various other little jobs. Soon the simple supper was ready, and Peter found that it tasted better than he expected. When the food was all eaten, the old man advised him to turn in right away. He was not at all unwilling to do so and in a few minutes was sound asleep a few feet from the fire. Uncle Seth sat smoking in silence.

When Peter awoke next morning, his friend was sitting in the same place and at first he thought that the old plainsman had spent the night on that log. But, looking about, he soon saw, not only that a brisk fire was burning, but also that Uncle Seth's blanket lay spread out nearby. He also discovered, to his great embarrassment, that practically all the chores had been attended to. When, however, he apologized for oversleeping, he was told cheerfully that he deserved a good long sleep and that he could get up first "to-morrer."

It took only a few minutes this time to eat breakfast and finish packing up, and in no time at all the little party was on its way, but not until its junior partner had learned more about living in the outdoors. He had had his rest, and Uncle Seth immediately impressed upon him that he had certain duties and that he would be held strictly to account for them. One of them was drinking coffee. Peter had never included that beverage in his diet. In fact, Mrs. Morris had preached many a sermon on the subject, assuring him that boys who drank coffee never grew to be big men. She had always talked as if he had wanted to drink it, whereas he would just as soon have swallowed a dose of castor oil. So far on this trip he had succeeded in sidestepping the ordeal, but that no longer was possible. When he tried to decline it, Uncle Seth informed him that he needed it to warm his "stummick," and ordered him to down some at once.

"Ye'll hev to drink sumthin' and I ain't takin' no cow along."

Peter repeated Mrs. Morris's admonitions, but they were dismissed with as much contempt as Uncle Seth would allow himself when a lady was involved. He would grow "plenty" on the Trail, and, if he didn't, he could start again when he reached Santa Fe. So there was nothing to do but pour in a liberal supply of brown sugar, make a face, and gulp. All these things Peter proceeded to do, adding a choking-fit for good measure. The taste was bitter and it lingered on his tongue. All morning he half expected to shrink to the size of a dwarf, but to his relief he found himself just as big at noon as he had been at six o'clock.

The other chores consisted of filling the canteens from the Big Blue Run—Uncle Seth surprised him by saying they would find no more water for miles—and helping with the saddling of the horses. Getting Blanky packed didn't take long, and at half-past six by Father Donahue's watch they were on their way.

The morning's ride was not very interesting. There were fewer farmhouses and the country was wilder, but no strange animals appeared and the whole landscape was monotonous. Uncle Seth had been right about the water. They saw none except in two unpleasant looking pools, which Peter was glad to pass by. Unfortunately, he expressed this sentiment aloud.

Uncle Seth replied with something like a snort. "Humph!," he exclaimed without turning around. "Someday ye may be glad to git a pull at sumthin' that's wuss'n thet. Ye'd better git over bein' so persnickety. Ye don't like coffee 'cause it's bitter, an' now ye turn up yer nose at a little puddle-water 'cause it's a mite scummy an' got some bugs swimmin' in it!"

Peter said nothing, but as he jogged along on Pluto, he had some unpleasant moments. Crossing the plains, he concluded, involved other things than fighting Indians.

During the morning they overtook several covered wagons filled with rough looking emigrants bound, according to Uncle Seth, for the camping-place known as "Lone Elm." There they would organize themselves into parties before starting the long, long trip to Oregon.

"Is that as far as Santa Fe?"

"A heap furtherer, a heap furtherer an' much harder. There's a sight o' them folks, Peter, young an' old, that won't never live to see the South

Pass, let alone Oregon. The hull trail's lined with graves."

"Do the Indians kill 'em?"

"Some, but not many. It's mostly sickness—cholera an' fever an' gittin' all tired an' wore out. Most of 'em don' hev no idea what they're agittin' into, an' won't listen to them thet tries to tell 'em. They'd be a sight better off at home, no matter how poor they wuz."

As they passed the great wagons with their loads of passengers—large, strong looking men, pale-faced women, and laughing children—Peter could not help shuddering at the thought that many would be left in lonely graves by the trail.

Shortly before noon, as they came over a rise of ground he was startled to see a great collection of these wagons drawn up near a tall, half-dead tree that stood by itself on a low hill. He had counted nearly fifty when his attention was attracted by the loud noise of men shouting and dogs yelping.

"Sounds like a Injun village," muttered Uncle Seth. Peter was soon to learn that Santa Fe traders had no high opinion of the emigrants who followed the road to the north.

When they came abreast of the nearest wagons, they were accosted by a man who tried to persuade them to "jine up," as he put it. He warned Uncle Seth of the hardships and perils of the Santa Fe Trail, assuming that the old man was a stranger and ignorant of the country. He himself had come from Illinois and had never before crossed the Plains. Peter was indignant and wanted to tell him that Uncle Seth knew more about both trails than the newcomer would ever learn, but he wisely decided to hold his tongue.

At this point, the rather one-sided conversation was interrupted by a fresh burst of yells from scores of throats and a pell-mell rush toward an open place on the other side of the dying elm. Without a word of farewell or anything but a prodigious "Halloo," the man left them and raced off after the others.

Now Peter saw something that made him open his eyes and mouth wide with amazement. Was it possible that these dozens of grown men, some of them with bushy beards, were playing a game of crack-the-whip? It was incredible; at home it was played only by children. Yet that certainly looked like what they were doing. They were seizing each other's hands and forming long lines, then rushing excitedly about the prairie in a bedlam of cheers and shouts. They were led by the men at the heads of the lines and ran this way and that, circling and bending back upon their own tracks. They called to men not yet attached to a chain to join their ranks and jeered at those who fell in with others. Some grew very angry, and two husky specimens got into a violent fistfight, cheered on by the members of their respective teams.

"What are they doing, Uncle Seth?"

"Holdin' a 'lection, sonny." His voice sounded sad.

"Holding an election!" The boy could hardly believe his ears.

"Yes, sir. They're choosin' leaders. The men who want the jobs is the ones in front. Looks like it's goin' to be close. An' prob'ly they don't know nuthin', either one of 'em. Don't make no difference though. In a couple o' weeks won't nobody mind 'em anyhow. Come on, Peter. Let's git goin'. We ain't voters." And he rode off.

"Say, you!" Peter heard a rough, metallic voice behind him, and turned in his saddle to see who was speaking. What he saw was a lanky, black-haired youth of about fifteen with the ugliest face he had ever seen glowering up at him. "I was talkin' to you."

The boy's tone made Peter angry. "Well, what of it?"

"Don't git sassy if you know what's good for you."

"I guess I know what's good for me all right. What do you want?"

"I want this." The youth stepped toward Pluto's side. "I want to know if this dirty yellow cur belongs to you."

"Yes," answered Peter hotly. He hastened to add, "He ain't dirty and he ain't a cur." The last statement made in Brownie's defense might well have been questioned.

"You'd better keep him away from my hound, or he'll be dead in five minutes. And don't you fergit it!"

Peter looked hurriedly about for Brownie and saw him standing a few feet away, head up, tail stiff, what there was of it, evidently on guard against a large, mangy black dog with a long thin tail that looked as if it had been broken near the end. The expression on his face was like his owner's, whom Peter thought of as the Ugly Boy.

"I'll forget it if I want to! He ain't hurtin' anybody!"

"Well, he better not try. If he gits funny, my hound'll eat him 'fore we've went ten mile!"

"Huh," scoffed Peter, "it would take more'n that to bother my dog! He's chewed up big dogs before now. I ain't scared, an' neither is he!" With that, he kicked his heels into Pluto's ribs. "Come on, Brownie!"

But the Ugly Boy jumped forward and seized the bridle. "Git down off'n that hoss afore I pull you off!" He reached for Peter's leg, but Pluto jerked away, and Brownie darted at his ankle, showing his teeth, threateningly and emitting growls that would have done credit to a dog twice his size. On the other hand, the black dog, not aware of the reputation given him by his owner, stayed at a safe distance.

"Git down off'n that hoss afore I pull you off!"

Starting Out on the Trail

At this moment Uncle Seth rode up, and the Ugly Boy, connecting him with Peter for the first time, slunk away in a hurry.

"Come on, Peter. Let's move on. We ain't a-goin' to Oregon."

"I'm glad," answered Peter. "And I'm glad he ain't goin' to Santa Fe."

So, carefully skirting the emigrant camp from which the sound of shouting and cheers still came, they once more headed for the West.

Before they had ridden very far, Peter, who kept a watchful eye on Brownie, decided that his friend looked tired. Consequently, he decided to see if he could convince him to become a horseman. He was a little afraid of the experiment, because if it did not work and Brownie leaped back to earth, he might easily break a leg. But the little dog looked weary, and his master felt he had no choice. So he stopped Pluto and, sliding to the ground, called his pet to him. Brownie, instead of standing on his hind legs, his forepaws against his master's side, lay down wearily and looked up pathetically. The next step was to get him into the saddle, something not easy to do without assistance. Peter stood so long trying to figure out a safe way to accomplish this that Uncle Seth missed him. Seeing what the trouble was, he turned Bonita's head and rode back.

"Little feller gittin' tired?" he asked.

"Yes, sir. I think he is," Peter replied.

"Wal, he ain't used to sech long marches yet." The old man dismounted. "Them feet is a mite sore, ain't they, Brownie?" he asked, scratching the small curly head. "Ye climb up on Pluto, an' I'll hand him up to ye. Reckon he's tired enough t' stay put."

Peter obeyed, and in a moment Brownie was settled in front of him in the saddle, where Uncle Seth admonished him to stay. Brownie had been born with more than his share of intelligence, from whatever assorted ancestors he may have inherited it, and always seemed to understand exactly what he was supposed to do. To his master's great relief, he settled down comfortably and made no effort to jump down. Soon they were on their way once more.

In a short time, they came to a fork in the road, and, reining in his horse, Uncle Seth pointed to a rough sign a little to the right.

"See thet sign?"

Peter peered at the weather-beaten post and with some difficulty was able to decipher the words Road to Oregon carved crudely in the wood.

"Thet's the way all them folks is goin'. See, thar's a wagon on ahead— somebody tryin' to make it alone." The old man shook his head and clucked to Bonita to move on.

On a rise a mile or so to the north, Peter could see the great canvas top of a single wagon outlined against the intense blue of the summer sky. As he watched, it passed over the crest of the hill and was swallowed up, as it seemed, by the ground. He looked after it in silence, his mind and imagination busy with the fate in store for the people in it. After a moment he dug his heels into Pluto's sides and followed Uncle Seth.

That day they traveled until dark and then camped under the stars on an open prairie. But they enjoyed none of the comforts of the night before. They had only the little wood Uncle Seth had picked up during the day and strapped onto Blanky's pack and a very small supply of water in their canteens. Peter shared his few drops with Brownie, but the horses had to do without. Uncle Seth said they had had several good drinks during the day and were used to being thirsty every now and then. For supper the unfortunate beasts had to be satisfied with some fresh grass he had gathered near the last creek they had passed. From Peter's point of view, however, there was one pleasing aspect of the situation. There would be no coffee in the morning.

That night he heard his first wolf. They had scarcely settled down in their blankets when out of the darkness that surrounded them there arose the most hair-raising sound he had ever heard or even dreamed of. Brownie growled and jumped to his feet. Peter sat up and strained his eyes trying to pierce the blackness of the night. The voice was deep and strong, and, as it rose and fell, it did strange things to his spine. Brownie backed up until his hind feet were against his master's knee, and from that safe spot he growled ominously, but not too loud—nor did he risk an out-and-out bark. Not being able to see anything at all and being extremely sleepy, Peter soon lay down again. Brownie tried to settle down too, but he kept getting up and then lying down, each time with a growl that seemed to say, "You'd better not bother me again." After a while, the wolf moved on to other hunting grounds, and Peter soon was lost in slumber. But first he decided that, after all, there was something reassuring about Uncle Seth's snores.

There followed another day like the last, except that they found more wood and water, especially at 110 Mile Creek, a deep narrow gash in the prairie with a sluggish stream of yellow water flowing through it. They rode on through heavy timber that gave them a little shelter from the scorching sun. The night was uneventful. No hungry wolf carried his investigations near enough to cause Brownie to do more than prick up his ears. At least, if any did, Peter was too sound asleep to hear the howls.

About noon the next day, just when his stomach was beginning to signal that lunchtime was at hand, Uncle Seth turned in his saddle and announced that they would not stop to eat, but would push right on to Council Grove. That was a blow, but Peter was so eager to move on that for a while his hunger was forgotten. Yet it did seem to him that they wouldn't reach the famous camping-ground before starvation set in. Then, just as he was about to swallow his pride and utter his first protest, there it was.

They came upon Council Grove so suddenly that he was taken by surprise. They were plodding along in the heat with nothing special to look at, the same rolling plain, the same sun-dried grass, the same withering cottonwoods—and then, all of a sudden, they had stopped on the edge of a hill and were looking down on a wide stream and, beyond it, a broad grove of oaks and walnuts. Dozens of columns of whitish smoke rose lazily from the grove of trees.

"Purty, ain't it?" exclaimed the old plainsman proudly. "Looks good from here, but nothin' like so good as when ye're comin' off'n the plains from the other direction an' ain't seen scarce a tree fer weeks or mebbe months. Look at it good. Ye won't see nuthin' like it fer a long, long time."

Peter did look. Among the trees he could see people moving to and fro and horses and oxen grazing—and even a small cabin. Half a dozen naked boys were bathing in the stream and shouting with joy. He wanted to run down the hill and jump in the water as he was.

"Let's go!" he cried excitedly.

"All right, Peter! No use a-waitin'! Giddap, Boniter! C'mon ye old white carcass of a Blanky! Brownie, let's tell 'em we're here!"

With that the old man let out a roar that nearly made Peter jump from his saddle and, waving his great hat above his head, started the outraged Bonita on a mad run down the hill. Blanky tried to hold back, but resistance was useless; he was pulled from the front and pushed from behind, for Peter was close at his heels, bouncing up and down on Pluto's back and shouting as loud as he could. Brownie was beside them, full of the spirit of the day and barking wildly as he ran.

Down the hill! Across the narrow strip of shore! Splash! One after another they plunged into the shallow water at the ford. In his excitement, his eyes fixed on the other side, Peter for once forgot his dog. Brownie, for his part, forgot all caution and plunged into the muddy water of the Neosho without stopping to investigate.

When they were halfway across, Peter remembered and glanced down for his pet. There was no Brownie to be seen. With a cry, he stopped Pluto in mid-stream and looked frantically about.

Far to the left, being borne swiftly with the current, he could just make out a little brown object almost the same color as the water, but surmounted by a white topknot.

"Brownie! Brownie!"

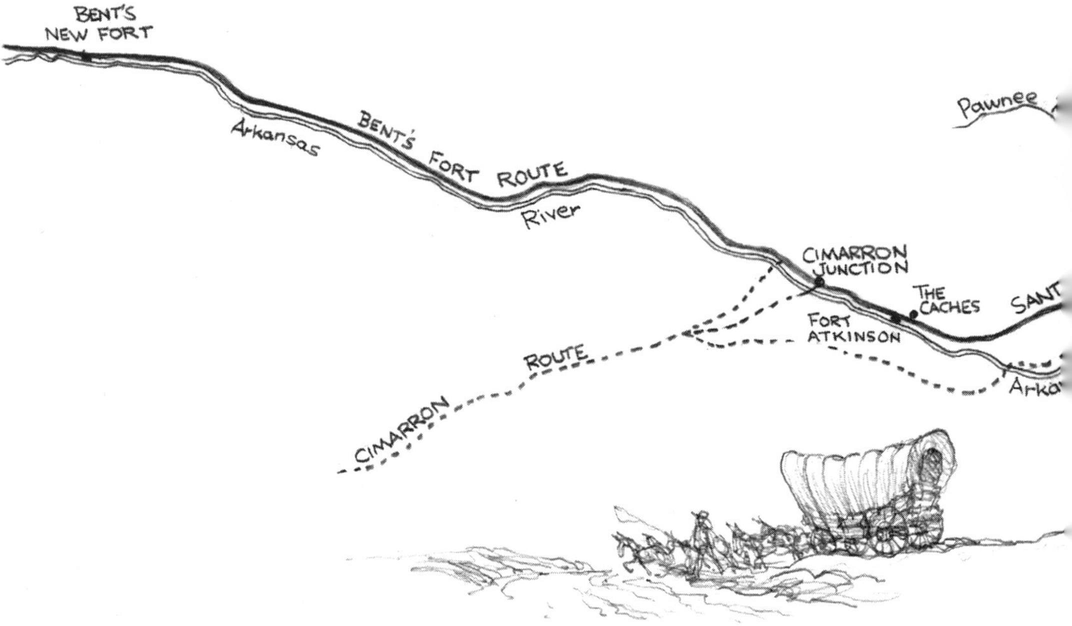

BENT'S
NEW FORT

Pawnee

Arkansas

BENT'S FORT ROUTE

River

CIMARRON
JUNCTION

THE
CACHES

SANT

FORT
ATKINSON

ROUTE

Arka

CIMARRON

Across the Trail to Bent's Fort

Walnut Creek

SH CREEK

PAWNEE
ROCK

RING

River

PAWNEE
FORK

TRAIL

Running Turkey Creek

COTTONWOOD
CROSSING

DIAMOND
SPRING

COUNCIL
GROVE

Neosho River

Santa Fe Trail ~ 1"=25 miles

8

"Catch Up! Catch Up!"

Frantic with fear, Peter swung Pluto to the left and kicked so hard that the startled horse responded with a leap forward that nearly jerked the rider from his saddle and did send his new hat sailing off into space.

"Brownie! Brownie!" he shouted again.

The stream was shallow, and Pluto ran ahead with greater speed than he usually made on dry land, kicking up quantities of yellow spray all about him. The noise quickly attracted drivers to the opposite shore, but Peter was not aware of the growing crowd. He had eyes for nothing but his lost pet. In a moment, to his intense relief, he saw the little dog emerge from the stream onto a narrow sandbar and stand there shaking himself in the sun. Pluto, however, kept right on, just as heedless of the uncertainty in the river as Brownie had been. The first thing he and Peter knew, he had stepped into a hole in the bottom of the stream, and down they both went. Fortunately the hole was neither deep nor large, and in a minute the astonished horse found his feet, and scrambled out onto the bar. It was a question who was the wettest—boy, horse, or dog.

Ignoring everything else, Peter slid from the saddle and knelt beside Brownie. The latter was apparently undisturbed. As a matter of fact, he had enjoyed the cool bath. Nevertheless, he was picked up and lifted to Pluto's back, where he obediently awaited his master. Peter grabbed his hat, which had floated onto the sand, clambered up, picked out an obviously shallow place, and lost no time in making his way to shore.

There he found an assorted and uproarious reception committee of men and boys who greeted him with a chorus of shouts and laughter.

"What's the matter? Cain't your dawg swim?"

Disconcerted as he was, Peter replied indignantly, "'Course he can! Didn't you see him?"

"Yuh acted like yuh thought he was gonna drownd," cried a large boy with a freckled face.

"Mebbe it ain't no dog—jest a cat," jeered an older man. "Lemme look at it."

Peter drew back. "Better not! He's liable to bite."

The man stopped and contented himself with peering from a safe distance, and exclaimed, "Thet's the funniest lookin' pup I ever see!"

He was probably right, because, if Brownie's appearance had been unique before, it was stranger now, bedraggled as he was. Moreover, he didn't enjoy being laughed at anymore than any other dog and looked sheepish and smaller than usual. Whether he showed it or not, his master felt sheepish too, realizing that he had just made a public display of himself.

Just then, however, he heard a voice he had heard before. "Here, lemme through! I've seen that dog before. It can't be there's two like him."

Peter turned, and there stood his friend from the levee, the big man whose hurrying wagon had almost knocked both Brownie and him to the Happy Hunting Ground. His eyes lit up with delight.

"Well, if it ain't the lad from St. Louis—Abel Blair's youngster! How in the name of all that's holy did ye get to this place?"

"He come with me, Aleck Cochran, you blue-nosed ole mule-handler. Any objections?"

There was Uncle Seth riding up on Bonita and leading the one-eyed Blanky.

All at once, Peter realized that Uncle Seth's absent partner was none other than his acquaintance of that afternoon on the riverfront. He wondered why the idea had never occurred to him before. He slid to the ground and lifted Brownie down after him. The arrival of the old man and his reunion with Aleck had distracted attention from Peter, and nobody was looking at him anymore. He was greatly relieved, but at the same time he was a little uneasy lest he might get another reprimand like the one that followed his behavior on the levee when he thought he was going to be left. But nothing was said. He was to learn in time that Uncle Seth knew when to scold and when not to, and also that nothing he did to help Brownie or one of the horses ever drew a rebuke.

After exchanging a few remarks with the men standing about, Uncle Seth observed that he would like "a mite o' somethin' to eat" and he reckoned Peter was "holler" too. "Holler" Peter certainly was—at least, he felt that that word described his condition perfectly.

Aleck took the hint at once and led the newcomers off in search of food. They followed a branch of the stream up to the ford, and then took a broad, well-trod road toward the west. Council Grove was a busy place. Everywhere Peter looked under the trees he saw covered wagons and their teams and large numbers of men and boys. He noticed that, in contrast to the camps of the Oregon parties, there were few women and children, indeed almost none. The men also were different, larger and darker. He had a feeling that they were more at home and knew better what they were doing than did the emigrants. There were few idlers. Most of the men were busy at many tasks and worked with obvious assurance and purpose. Their job was to get manufactured goods to New Mexico to sell or trade.

Once more, Peter was impressed by the number of them who hailed his guardian either by name or some facetious nickname. He decided quickly that the old fellow must be very popular. To every greeting the latter responded cheerily, usually with a wave of his huge right hand and a hearty "halloo." There was certainly no trace here of the awkward embarrassment that had marked his behavior in Mrs. Morris's parlor.

It took only a short time to reach Aleck's camp. There Peter recognized at once the very wagon whose mad rush down the levee had preceded this great adventure. But it no longer suggested a staveless barrel on wheels, for its top was resplendent with a covering of new canvas. The trip up the river to Independence and across the prairie had in no way dimmed its splendid newness, for it still shone as if the paint had scarcely dried. Moreover, the white top seemed to Peter to have increased its size. He felt very small as he stood beside it. In his eyes there was no other wagon like it on the Trail—and there never would be.

Chapter Eight

In the brief look he had had on the levee in St. Louis he had not had a chance to peer inside. Now he did so and discovered that it was crammed full of all sorts of things. He could not tell what they were, because almost all of them were wrapped carefully in canvas.

He was told that Uncle Seth had, for the time being at least, switched from trapping to trading, and in partnership with Mr. Cochran, was taking a load of St. Louis merchandise to sell in Santa Fe. He did not think trading was nearly as glamorous as trapping, but maybe, he concluded, Uncle Seth was getting a little too old for the kind of roughing it he had described so vividly in Mrs. Morris's parlor and on the boat. And, after all, his father worked in a store.

While wandering about the camp, he made still another discovery that caused him a great deal of surprise. He found Mr. Cochran watering not two, but eight mules.

"Mr. Cochran, what you doin' with eight mules?"

"My name's Aleck," answered his friend. "I ain't old enough to be 'mistered.' Two mules ain't enough to haul this load to Santa Fe, as you'll soon find out if you stick with Seth 'n me. Could use more just in case the Indians run some of 'em off, but I'll take a chance—now that we've got you and Brownie to keep 'em from gettin' too close."

"What's in all those packages in the wagon?"

Aleck took time to hit at a hungry mosquito on his nose. But he had been too slow, and now he scratched the bite before he answered. "Your bump o' curiosity ain't exactly small, is it?"

Peter was embarrassed, but before he could apologize, the Scotsman went on.

"That's a good thing, sonny. That's a good way to find out aboot things, and there's lots o' things you'll need to learn before we go very far. Those packages have got things in 'em that we plan to sell to the people in Santa Fe. They're things they want and can't find there— pots, dishes, furniture, clothes, wine—all kinds of things. They don't have many stores like the ones in St. Louis, an', if it weren't for what traders like us bring 'em over the Trail, they'd just plain have to go without."

There were more questions Peter would have liked to ask, but he was

95

a little taken aback and watched silently as Aleck finished his job.

"I'll be glad to water the mules for you," he volunteered, for he was eager to be helpful.

Aleck accepted this offer in short order. "Listen, sonny, there won't be many times you'll have a chance to. Water ain't exactly plentiful on the Trail, an' these old buzzards'll have some pretty thirsty days. But they're used to that. It's a mighty poor mule that can't go a couple o' days without a drink."

In a few minutes he had finished giving the animals what Peter feared was their last drink. Aleck turned to the boy.

"Come on, young'un, time for grub."

Aleck was a generous host. He lost no time in filling the stomachs of his guests. From a far corner of the wagon he produced a loaf of bread—somewhat stale—and several pieces of dried meat and soon was busy over the fire Uncle Seth had kindled. Peter was very hungry, and the smells emanating from the skillet made his mouth water. But there was something else that had a different effect. Resting uncertainly on two burning logs was a pot of coffee, which produced sounds and odors that brought back unpleasant memories. He could not help wishing that one of the logs would burn away more quickly than was expected, thus removing for the time being this particular menace. But the hope was faint and, he was sure, futile, for he knew that Uncle Seth would brew some more of the villainous stuff with the greatest possible speed. So he resigned himself to his fate and tried to smell nothing but the meat.

This time, however, fate was on his side. Somehow Aleck seemed to sense his state of mind.

"Mebbe the lad's not got a fancy for coffee like us old'uns. How'd a cup of milk taste, Peter?"

The boy held his breath. Surely Uncle Seth would interfere, but the old man merely busied himself with the sizzling skillet and said nothing.

"Yes, sir, I would—very much. I haven't had any since we left Independence."

The milk, when he got it, was lukewarm and only a day from turning sour, and for a minute he thought he couldn't swallow it, but it was better than the detested coffee. If he had known that this was the last milk that was to come his way for many weeks, he would have been very much depressed. The rest of the meal consisted of the meat that smelled so good, bread, and pickles. Peter was hungry enough to enjoy everything. Mrs. Morris had carefully packed a fork, a knife, and a couple of spoons so that he could mind his manners on the Plains, but when he saw how his companions were stowing away their food, he quickly concluded that manners on the Trail were not the same as manners on Fourth Street, and acted accordingly. Uncle Seth and Aleck just cut off hunks of beef with their hunting knives and conveyed them to their mouths with their great calloused fingers. Peter followed their example, and as he did so, got a certain satisfaction out of imagining the expression on Mrs. Morris's face if she could have seen him.

By the time supper was eaten, his eyelids were so heavy that he feared he would have to hold them open with his fingers if he wanted to stay awake. He waited uncomfortably for the moment when he could ask permission to crawl in between his blankets.

He was only dimly aware that the group about the fire had been joined by two newcomers. But, just as he was about to fall off his log, he was jolted back to consciousness by the turn taken by the conversation.

"Which way you figgerin' on takin'?" asked one of the visitors.

"Dry," replied Uncle Seth.

The stranger merely grunted.

"Any objections?"

"Lots o' Comanches. They're lookin' fer to whip some Pawnees huntin' buffalo, but their fingers is itchin' fer hosses an' scalps. They wouldn't care much whose they were. White man's 'd do jest as well. I figger they've collected a few already, an' a few more wouldn't make 'em feel bad. Like to do a little kidnapping, too. We bumped into about twenty down by McNees Creek, an' if there hadn't been s'many of us, we could o' had a fight, but they thought their hides 'd be safer somewhere else, an' went on off. We figgered we'd be better off somewheres else too, an' moved on 'thout stoppin' to look at the scenery. 'Taint very healthy down 'roun' there this summer."

"Catch Up! Catch Up!"

"Thet's the way we wuz thinkin' 'bout goin'," said Uncle Seth. "Lot shorter 'n the Raton."

"Wal, you know yer own bizness."

By this time even the thought of Comanches was scarcely enough to keep Peter conscious during the long silence that followed, and he was about to ask permission to go to bed when he was startled wide awake by the words 'Abel Blair.'

Peter sat upright.

"Seen him lately?"

"Yep, I seen Abel jest a couple o' days 'fore I left Santa Fe—in Spiegelberg's shop." Here he took time out to squirt a stream of tobacco juice into the coals.

"Still clerkin' there?"

"Was. But God knows where he is by this time."

Peter felt a chill run down his spine.

"Goin' somewhere?"

The man was in no hurry. Now he took time out to fish in his pocket and pull out a plug of tobacco. He cut off a large piece which he put in his mouth and began to chew.

Peter could take no more. "Where is he going?" he demanded shrilly.

The man slowly shifted his gaze to the boy, whom he seemed not to have noticed before. He looked him over slowly. But he finally decided to answer.

"I can't rightly remember—didn't pay much attention—Californy prob'ly. Thet's where most ever'body's headin' these days."

Peter turned cold all over and began to shake.

Aleck reached over and put a large hand on his shoulder. "Steady there, lad. Better sit down a minute." He gently pushed him down onto the log from which he had just sprung and then turned back to the stranger. "This here's Abel's boy. Goin' out to Santa Fe to join his Pa."

"Wal, mebbe he'll still be there. Mebbe."

Peter didn't know that he was not the only one dismayed by the news. Uncle Seth also suffered a shock. When he had agreed to take Peter to Santa Fe, it had never occurred to him that they might not find Abel where he had left him, behind the counter in Spiegelberg's shop. He was almost as appalled as his charge. He had not reckoned with the possibility that he might find himself in New Mexico with a twelve-year-old boy on his hands.

"Abel say he was headin' fer Californy?"

"Don't remember." The stranger obviously did not consider the matter of much importance. He slowly rose to his feet and stretched. "C'mon, Jim, time to turn in." And his companion, who had not opened his lips during the visit, followed him without a word.

Uncle Seth sat silent on his log. He had plenty to think about, and at the moment he was thinking none too kindly of the boy who had gotten him into this fix.

Peter wanted to speak to him, and he even started to do so, but something in the old man's expression told him this was not the time. So he sat still.

"C'mon, lad, time to hit the hay." Aleck, sensing the situation, pulled him up by the arm and pushed him toward the place where his blankets lay beneath a tree. "Some folks talk too much. Jake ain't got much sense. Likely it wasn't Abel he was talkin' to. Anyway, if it was, we'll find him somewheres. Don't you worry. Go to sleep an' fergit the whole bizness." He pulled Peter's boots off and threw the blankets over him. "Now do like I say. Ever'thing'll look better in the mornin'." Even Brownie seemed worried as he crawled under the blankets.

Aleck's advice was sensible and well intended, but under the circumstances it was not easy to follow. Peter was terrified and for the second time he was overcome with homesickness. For a few minutes he lay still. Then a wolf began its mournful howl, and in a tree nearby an owl began hooting. This was too much, and the boy began to sob miserably. He could not help it. Then he felt a hand on his shoulder, and, opening his eyes, he saw that Aleck had returned and was sitting on the ground beside him. The man said nothing, but lit his pipe and smoked in silence. In a little while Peter dropped off to sleep.

The next thing he knew, it was broad daylight, the wolf had gone about his business, and the owl had finished whatever he had had to say. Instead, there were wild sounds of shouting and cursing all about him. He jumped to his feet and saw on every side that men were hitching teams of mules or sleepy looking oxen to their wagons.

"Hello, Peter! Come over and fill up that stummick o' yours. It must be about empty, an' warm yerself with some nice hot coffee." Aleck sounded so cheerful that at first Peter thought he must have had a bad dream and really had no trouble in the world. But the sight of Uncle Seth sitting glumly by the fire, silently gulping down his coffee, dispelled that pleasant illusion. The old man had not spoken to him since the bad news had been broken the night before, and he was afraid to say anything himself, for he could feel in his bones that he was not exactly in favor. Even Brownie, warned by some sixth sense, kept a respectful distance and stayed close to his master's feet.

To his great relief, however, Uncle Seth grunted and muttered, "Hustle yerself some grub."

Peter did as he was told. There was no milk this morning, and there was nothing to do but swallow a cup of coffee. It tasted vile, but it was hot, and, after he had succeeded in getting it down and eating some fried ham and dry bread, he found he felt better and that things did not look as dismal as they had the night before. Aleck produced some scraps for Brownie—and in a minute or two the world seemed much better.

Uncle Seth moved about gathering up the breakfast dishes. "Here, Peter," he commanded, "you can clean up these here plates, an' then roll up yer blankets, an' tie 'em on yer hoss." Seeing the boy look about for some water, he added. "Don't waste yer time lookin' fer water. There's some sand over thar. It'll do jest as well. You'll have to git over yer fancy ways."

Peter had never heard of washing dishes with sand, but thought he had better not say so and went to work rubbing with all his strength. He was surprised to see how well the substitute worked and wondered what Mrs. Morris would say if she heard washing dishes with water called "fancy ways."

"Now take 'em," Uncle Seth directed when he had finished, "an' put 'em in the wagon."

When he did so, he found Aleck hitching up his mules. He watched the process with much curiosity until he was told to "get that nag o' yers ready to hit the trail. Better water him first. And fill yer canteen as full as it'll hold, an' yer belly too. It's goin' to be hot, an' ye'll be dry before we've gone a mile. But don't drink any till you have to. Ye'll be needin' all the water you c'n get."

So the boy led his pony down to the stream, where he drank all the water he could hold. Peter, after filling the canteen, drank a prodigious amount himself. It worried him that he could not persuade Brownie to follow his example, but consoled himself with the thought that probably the little dog had visited the creek earlier.

When he returned to the wagon, he found Uncle Seth there too, tightening the cinches on his saddle. He plainly was not restored to his usual good humor, for he turned on Peter and demanded crossly to know why he had not saddled Pluto.

"I sent him down to the creek to water the nag an' fill his canteen," Aleck shouted over the noise.

As he started to obey orders, Peter began to feel miserable again, especially when he found himself faced with a problem that, try as he would, he could not solve. The saddle was very heavy, and he simply could not lift it into place. Every morning before this Uncle Seth had done the hoisting for him, but this morning he apparently was not going to help. After a few minutes, however, seeing that the boy was doing his utmost, he silently lifted it up onto Pluto's back. Then he walked away without acknowledging Peter's murmured thanks.

The noise about them was overwhelming. It seemed that every man in the camp was shouting and yelling at the top of his lungs. "Catch up! Catch up!" The men had almost finished hitching their teams to the great wagons. Oxen were hitched to most instead of mules. He was shocked by the way these poor, uncomplaining beasts were struck and kicked, and he was glad Mrs. Morris was not there to hear the language these rough men used.

He soon learned that Uncle Seth and Aleck were joining a party for safety's sake and that the former had been chosen leader. He also remembered what he had been told about the way the other drivers soon got into the habit of ignoring the orders of the man they had elected their leader.

There was something else he discovered that caused him much greater concern—the Ugly Boy was to be a member of the same party! He caught a glimpse of his dirty blue shirt among the wagons. His presence, Peter did not need to be told, boded no good for Brownie, but there was nothing he could do except be on his guard and try to keep his pet in sight.

Before long the wagons had been maneuvered into line with Aleck's in the lead. To his dismay another mule-drawn vehicle came next, and he soon saw that the Ugly Boy was with the rough looking men who owned it, and who contributed more than their fair share to the cursing indulged in by the whole company. The Ugly Boy was mounted on a scraggly looking white pony—at least, Peter supposed it had once been white— and kept abreast of the wagon, where it was to be hoped he would stay.

Uncle Seth on Bonita rode on ahead of the caravan, leading his packhorse. Peter rode up beside him, partly to see if he could get back in his good graces and partly to get as far away as he could from undesirable company. Neither one spoke.

Brownie, who did not seem to have a worry in the world, ran on ahead, trying to catch at least one of the little prairie dogs who sat up everywhere the eye could see, but he had no luck, for when they saw him coming, they bolted down into their holes, leaving a sorely mystified little dog to wonder what had become of them.

The country was now very flat with short grass and almost no trees. Frustrated by the elusive prairie dogs and finding little else to interest him, Brownie soon returned to his master and trotted along beside Pluto. Thinking that he might be tired and wishing to keep him out of harm's way, Peter scrambled down and lifted him up onto the saddle, where he joined him in a minute, and the two of them rode on in comfort. Peter forgot his troubles for the time being.

Before they had gone very far in this fashion, Uncle Seth called, "Peter!" and motioned for him to pull up alongside him. He pointed with his whip to a tan animal shaped something like a deer with a white rump and stubby black horns off to the right of the road.

"What is it?" Peter asked.

"Antelope."

Just then the black dog, barking wildly, and with the Ugly Boy after him on his dirty white pony, dashed toward the antelope. But almost before they had started, their intended prey disappeared.

"Durn fool!" muttered Uncle Seth, "thinkin' he could ketch thet critter! If thet cur don't look out, one o' them wolves'll chaw him up. Then he won't pester Brownie no more. Wish they would!"

For the first time Peter spotted several of these gaunt animals skulking in the distance. They were so nearly the color of the ground that he had not noticed them before.

After this slight excitement, the day passed uneventfully. The party halted for lunch near a large pool that Uncle Seth called "Diamond Spring." Peter got a chance to help Aleck water the mules, for it was less trouble to fill and carry large buckets to them than it would have been to unhitch them and then harness them to the wagon again. To his indignation, he saw that the rough looking men in the second wagon did not bother to give their animals any water, but beat them unmercifully when they tried to reach the spring. Instead, the men spent their time quarreling among themselves. Peter noticed that both Uncle Seth and Aleck glared at them.

The party started again after lunch and kept on its slow way. To Peter, who was impatient to get on, this slowness was exasperating, especially as the landscape was monotonous, and he had become used to the ever-present wolves and prairie dogs. As far as he could see, it was the same—flat and uninteresting. The terrible heat was another thing. But there was nothing he could do except put up with all of it and keep a watchful eye on Brownie.

They plodded on in silence until well after dark. Then all the wagons, except the second one, pulled some distance from the road and halted for the night. The mules were unhitched, but the men put hobbles on their front feet to keep them from straying far. Uncle Seth and Aleck eyed the drivers of the second wagon with open disgust. In fact, the latter walked over and advised them to pull closer to the rest. He returned in short order, however, to report that they had told him to mind his own business. "Never been on the Plains before, but they know better than those that have crossed 'em twenty times. Well, if the Comanches don't get their scalps, the Pawnees will."

That night the men took turns standing guard. Uncle Seth said there was not much danger yet, but their mules and ponies would look good to the "Injuns" and some might try to help themselves to a few. Peter wanted to take a turn, but Aleck said:

"That's man's work, Pete, and you're just a mite too young, though I'd a heap rather risk my hide with you than with some trash I know."

"Looks like rain, Peter," said Uncle Seth. "You'd best sleep under the wagon. And," he added, "tie Brownie to one o' the wheels so thet he won't go sky-larkin' off after one o' them wolves. They like dog meat jest about as much as the Injuns do."

Peter did as he was told. Brownie did not relish the arrangement, for he was not used to being tied up, but his master laid his blanket close to the wheel and they snuggled down comfortably together. As it turned out, it did not rain, but the wind blew very hard. Apparently the mosquitoes, which otherwise would have been blown back to Independence, all took refuge under the wagon and nearly drove Peter to distraction until he finally fell asleep from exhaustion.

The next day was much the same as the last. The heat was awful, and they had only enough water for tantalizing sips. Peter, when he thought no one was looking, gave Brownie a little—a very little—from his own tin cup. Just as he was putting the cup away, he became aware that Uncle Seth was watching him and braced himself for a dressing-down, but nothing was said, and he climbed back into his saddle and lost himself in his thoughts.

But there was an unexpected thrill—or at least excitement—just around the corner. He saw his first buffalo. At first he did not realize what they were because they were about half a mile from the trail, and because the great black beasts did not seem to be moving, he mistook them for rocks. Suddenly he was awakened from his daydreaming by loud shouts and wild barking, and he saw the Ugly Boy dashing madly off on his pony with his dog yelping ahead. The "rocks" lumbered slowly off, but the pursuit continued. This was too much for Brownie. The ancestral hunting blood coursing in his veins began to boil, and he tore off pell-mell after his bitter enemies.

"Best ketch 'im," warned Uncle Seth, and Peter, whipping Pluto unmercifully and shouting, "Brownie! Brownie!" at the top of his voice, raced off after the others. The buffalo having galloped away, the Ugly Boy spotted Brownie and headed his horse for him. He "sicked" the black cur on him, and for a moment things looked bad. But fortunately Uncle Seth came riding up at full speed, and the Ugly Boy suddenly decided he had business to attend to somewhere else.

When they regained the road, Uncle Seth said emphatically, "You an' Brownie best leave buffalo alone. Yer liable to git into trouble."

About noon black clouds began to pile up in the west. Uncle Seth and Aleck decided that they had better push on and try to get across Cottonwood Crossing before the going got too bad. The former rode back along the line of wagons and passed along word that there would be no noon halt. But their haste was in vain. The slow-plodding oxen just could not go any faster. Of course the men in the second wagon would not cooperate. Lashing their unfortunate mules furiously, they drove past Aleck and caught up with Uncle Seth and Peter on their horses.

"Hey there, what you doin'?" the old man shouted.

But they ignored him except to hurl a volley of curses at him, and in the deepening darkness were soon almost out of sight.

Peter thought he had never seen such inky black clouds as now filled the western sky, and he probably never had. Again and again, the wagons and riders were lit up by flashes of lightning—the roar of the thunder grew louder and louder while the wind screamed over the Plains. He had to hang on to his hat. Then he could see a curtain of rain advancing toward them. Before he knew it, they were engulfed by a deluge, first rain, then the biggest hailstones he had ever seen. In front of him on the saddle, Brownie, terrified and hurt, began to whimper, and Peter tucked him in under his coat as best he could. They now were in the midst of flashing lightning and deafening crashes of thunder. Brownie was not the only one who was frightened—his owner was, too. Indeed the whole company had good reason to be, for they made open targets for the lightning. It was all over in a few minutes, but it left them drenched, and the road, which had been deep in dust, was now little more than a quagmire. The wheels of the carts slid and then got stuck in the ruts worn by the hundreds of wagons that had preceded them over the years.

It was often beyond the power of the oxen, straining as hard as they could, to move the wagons, and time and again the men had to put their shoulders to the wheels and push for all they were worth. But not the drivers of the second wagon. They had driven on ahead and somehow or other, Peter feared with good reason, had managed to keep moving by cruelly lashing their poor mules.

They could, however, move only so far and no farther. Long before the others reached Cottonwood Crossing, they could hear the two men yelling and cursing. Peter shuddered at the sound of blows being rained down on their unfortunate animals.

The creek had through the years cut a channel deep in the prairie between the trees which grew along its banks. The banks were not steep, but the downpour had made them very slippery. The drivers had apparently tried to get up the far side at top speed, only to have one of their mules lose its footing and fall, causing their wagon to slide sideways across the track. Knowing nothing else to do, they were punishing their animals for their stupidity.

Uncle Seth was the first to reach the scene. "Stop beatin' them mules!" he shouted angrily.

"Shut your big mouth," one of the men replied. "They're our mules, an' we'll beat 'em to death if we've a mind to!"

"It ain't their fault. It's yers, you big fools! Beatin' the poor critter ain't gonna git 'im up."

The two men were in a rage, and it looked for a minute as if there were going to be a fight, but several of the teamsters came up, and the two thought better of it and contented themselves with cursing under their breaths. Peter caught several glimpses of the Ugly Boy, but he kept in the background.

Uncle Seth went up to the fallen mule and, talking to it quietly, succeeded in getting it back on its feet. Then with several of the teamsters, he set about shoving the wagon back onto the path. Seeing the Ugly Boy, he angrily ordered him to lend a hand, but, instead, he fled back into the shadows. Peter volunteered his services, but was sent back to hold Aleck's mules. The job of getting all the wagons across the creek and up the other side consumed most of the night, but eventually it was accomplished, and, after a cup of coffee, everybody settled down for what remained of the darkness.

But not for long. In a little while they were all awakened by the sound of frantic barking. In an instant all were on their feet preparing for an attack. To his chagrin and alarm, Peter found that Brownie had slipped his leash and taken off on what he thought to be his own affairs. There could be no doubt who was making the noise. Fortunately it turned out to be a false alarm, and to his master's great mortification—but not his own—the little dog, instead of being a hero, was in disgrace.

After breakfast, when Peter was riding along with the culprit at Pluto's side, he ran into the Ugly Boy.

"That good-fer-nuthin' cur o' yourn woke ever'body up fer nuthin'."

"He thought he saw an Indian."

"Indian!" answered the boy scornfully. "There ain't an Indian in a hunderd miles."

"Ain't there?" answered Peter hotly. "Your hound wouldn't know one if he saw one. He'd let us all get scalped in our sleep!"

"Well, he won't wake me up no more! I'll fix 'im!" With that, he drew a large pistol from his belt, and aimed it at Brownie.

With a cry, Peter leaped to the ground and struck the dirty arm holding the pistol. There was a loud report followed by a canine shriek of anguish. Peter was terrified, but a quick look showed that his own pet was intact while the black dog was limping about with a bleeding foreleg.

The beast's owner gave way to uncontrolled rage. He began furiously reloading his pistol, at the same time pouring out a flow of profanity which out-did even his father's efforts. Before anything more serious could happen, Uncle Seth, who had ridden off some little distance, came galloping back and took a hand in the affair. He was off his horse in a second and, seizing the Ugly Boy by the back of his neck, shook him so hard that his teeth rattled—he dropped the pistol.

"Any more trouble out o' you, an' I'll thrash yer hide off clean through your britches, an' leave you fer wolf-bait!" he roared. "It's natural fer boys to fight with their fists, but when they start with guns, it's time to

107

"Catch Up! Catch Up!"

"Well, he won't wake me up no more!
I'll fix 'im!"

use a switch! You leave thet little dog alone! Now git!"

He ended the shaking with such a shove that the boy sprawled forward on his face.

He crawled to his knees and reached for his weapon, but Uncle Seth grabbed it first and hurled it as far away as he could. The boy scrambled to his feet and ran off, stopping at a safe distance to scream back imprecations and threats of revenge. That done to his satisfaction, he made himself scarce as fast as he could.

"I hadn't orter done that," said Uncle Seth after a few minutes.

"Done what?" Peter asked.

"Throwed his gun away like I did. Ever'body needs a gun on the Trail. But he made me so mad I didn't think whut I wuz doin'. But he's so ornery like as not he'd a shot one of us 'stead of an Injun. Mebbe he'll find it. Keep yer eyes peeled fer it." And he himself eyed the ground carefully.

Just then a great uproar arose ahead of them, and the two men with the Ugly Boy came running up.

"I'll kill you fer treatin' my boy like you done!" yelled one of them.

"Go ahead!" replied Uncle Seth, "but you better learn him not to fool aroun' with his gun thet-a way. If anybody gits killed 'roun' here, mebbe it won't be me."

By this time several of the teamsters came crowding about—and made it clear whose side they were on.

"I seen 'im go fer to shoot the little dog!" cried one. "He got jest whut was a-comin' to him."

Seeing that the odds were against him, the man changed his tune. But he exclaimed, "I'm sick o' this rotten outfit. The way we're travelin', we'll never git to Santa Fe."

"The oxen are makin' as good time as they can."

"They'd go fast enough if you'd whup 'em."

"Nobody's goin' to whip my team," put in a tall young man. "Them wagons is heavy."

"Wal, I ain't gonna poke along with this outfit no more. I'm pushin' ahead on my own time. We'll be in Santa Fe afore you git to Fort Atkinson."

"Better not," said Aleck, who had not spoken before.

"Why not?"

"This here is Indian country. If your scalps mean anythin' to you, you'd better stick close to us."

The man spat contemptuously. "Injuns! You all are so skeered, you can't sleep nights! Wal, I ain't skeered of 'em. Anyway, there ain't none of 'em aroun'! We're pushin' on."

The others added more warnings, but the pair turned their backs and walked off. In a few minutes they were again whipping their mules, and their wagon moved on ahead alone.

9

Brownie Becomes a Hero

After a little while the whole party got under way, the wagons traveling four abreast. The clouds had disappeared; so the sun beat down cruelly on the parched plain. The heat was deadly, and soon everybody was suffering from thirst. The oxen seemed to be worse off than the mules. Peter kept Brownie on the saddle in front of him, but the poor little dog whimpered. This made his master feel worse, but there was nothing he could do. They rode this way for hours.

Suddenly somebody shouted, "Buffalo!" Sure enough, in the distance to the right of the road Peter saw an enormous herd of the huge beasts galloping toward them. It looked for a minute as if they would run over the wagons, but the first of them went around and galloped on.

"Injuns is runnin' 'em!" somebody shouted. The men scanned the plain to the north, but saw none.

"They smell water somewheres," said Uncle Seth.

The fear of Indians having been banished, a number of the men rode off in pursuit, and soon there was the sound of volleys of shots. Peter had had visions of himself bravely bringing down a great bull, but now he was too miserable to do anything but sit tight in his saddle. Besides, there was Brownie. He was in no shape to run on the hot ground, and, if he had been, he would have been trampled to death. As it was, Peter soon had seen enough. The great brutes still lumbered by, and the men who shot at them could hardly miss. One after another fell to the ground, some of them killed at once, others struggling to get to their feet again, blood gushing from their mouths. The sight of so much slaughter sickened the city-bred boy, who had never imagined anything like this. He grew faint and had to cling to the pommel of his saddle to keep from falling off Pluto's back. When he did open his eyes, he saw the men cutting off great hunks of meat and stuffing it into their mouths raw.

He quickly shut his eyes again, but then heard his name and opened them. There was Uncle Seth standing beside him with a piece of bloody meat held out for him to take. The world went black and he swayed from side to side. If there had been anything in his stomach, he would have thrown up.

"Swaller some o' this, an' you'll be all right."

All Peter could do was shake his head miserably.

Fortunately, rescue was at hand in the shape of Aleck. "Leave the boy be. If he did swaller it, he couldn't keep it down, an' it wouldn't do him no good."

Uncle Seth was plainly disgusted. "Let 'im go thirsty then! How's he think he c'n cross the Plains if he's too proud to eat a little raw meat? I'll bet Brownie ain't so persnickety." He lifted the little dog down, and Brownie quickly proved that he was right.

Then he took himself off.

"Don't you mind Seth. He's so used to this sort o' thing, he can't understand anybody who's not. Here, lad, drink this." The kindly Scotsman produced his canteen and held it to Peter's mouth. "Don't drink too much. It's all I've got to last till God knows when."

Obediently, despite the temptation to drink more, Peter did little more than moisten his lips and tongue. The water was sickeningly warm, but it was welcome. Thanking Aleck in a faint voice, he handed back the canteen.

"Jest remember, laddie," admonished his benefactor, "you'll have to do lots o' things you don't like if you want to see your Pa in Santa Fe. An' remember this too—you was the one who asked to make this trip. Seth didn't drag you along."

"I'm sorry," murmured the boy, blinking back the tears. "I just couldn't help it. It made me sick to my stomach."

No sooner had the men had their fill of meat than the slow journey was resumed. All were refreshed, including Brownie, except Peter, who

Chapter Nine

remained utterly wretched in mind and body and rode on scarcely aware of his surroundings. At last, however, he was conscious that they had reached what he heard one of the men call "Running Turkey Crick." This proved to be a dry streambed with a few bushes on either side, but the wagon stopped. Peter managed to climb off Pluto and stagger a few steps before he sank down to the ground, the picture of misery.

Soon he heard a fire crackling, and in a little while Uncle Seth came up to him with a slab of partly cooked meat. "Here," he said gently, "mebbe you'll like this better. It's been on the fire some, but you need the juice." After a bite or two Peter found that it tasted surprisingly good, and, when he had downed it all, he felt much better. He knew he had to get used to this diet, because, except for crackers and pickles, he was to know little else for some time to come. Not even the hated coffee was forthcoming; there was seldom enough water to make it.

That night, for the first time, the wagons were arranged to form a corral, that is in a circle with the front of each one touching the rear of another. This was for defense against attack. All the animals were supposed to be hitched up inside the circle, but this was not a large train and there was not space for all of them. So the ponies and mules were collected in the corral, and most of the slow-moving oxen, in which the Indians would not be so interested, were fastened outside, relying on the guards to protect them. To get out from under foot, Peter and Brownie crawled under the wagon. He was glad he had done so, for it turned considerably cooler and before long he heard the welcome sound of rain. He heard something else too, beside the nightly howling of the wolves, something he was unable to identify. In the morning Aleck explained that it had been the bellowing of the buffalo bulls, a sound as welcome as the patter of the rain, for it meant that there were probably no Indians prowling about.

The next few days were not as bad as the preceding ones. The sky was overcast from time to time and, not only was it not so hot, but a few sprinkles supplied them with a little water. The grass was also longer and greener; consequently great herds of buffalo were reassuringly present and supplied plenty of fresh meat.

They crossed a number of streams, some with difficulty, not because they were full of water, which they were not, but because the banks were steep, and the patient oxen were hard put to drag the heavily laden wagons back up to level ground. The names of these streambeds made little impression on Peter, but he did "sit up and take notice" when after several days, they came to the low sandy banks of a broad shallow river which he was told was the famous Arkansas.

All of a sudden Uncle Seth reined Bonita in to a dead stop and peered intently to the south shading his eyes against the sun.

"Comanches!" he exclaimed.

The whole train halted, and everyone stared across the river.

"Don't see none."

"I seen a couple, but they've hid 'mselves behind somethin'. They're thar all right." No one questioned his word. "We'll halt this side o' the Walnut," he added. "We don't want to git cotched among all them trees an' bushes."

The march was resumed, but everyone was on the alert and constantly scanned the horizon on all sides. Before they had gone very far, Peter made out far ahead a dark line which he took to be the trees bordering Walnut Creek. It was only mid-afternoon, but Uncle Seth called a halt, and the wagons were wheeled into their night formation. The men carefully checked their guns, and the guards took up places close to the wagons. There was no wood and no fires—nor was there any water. As soon as darkness fell, Aleck told Peter to go to bed under the wagon, and, whatever happened, not to raise his head. As usual, he tied Brownie to the wheel beside him. He tried his best to stay awake, but in a few minutes was fast asleep.

Sometime during the night, he was awakened by the sharp crack of a gun and could tell by what he heard that the men had sprung to their feet. Nothing more was heard, however, and everybody settled down again. When he woke up, it was daylight and the men were grimly hitching up. He asked one of the drivers what had happened.

"Oh, Ben pro'bly seen a wolf or a buffalo. Whatever it was, he missed. Anyway, the buffalo is back. So 'taint likely it was a Injun."

Although nothing would have been easier for an Indian than to shoot a steak on the hoof, the grazing oxen had not been molested during the night.

"They're waitin' fer us at the Walnut, hidin' out in them bushes," someone volunteered. "Thet's a bad place, but there's nuthin' to do but face the music."

In less time than Peter would have thought possible the train was moving ahead, slowly and cautiously. However, he was not in his accustomed place, astride Pluto and close to Uncle Seth. Instead, he was in the wagon with Brownie behind Aleck who was driving the team while riding the left rear mule as he always did. He had known this might happen and, so, had moved three boxes of freight to make a place for Peter to sit and Brownie to lie. He had also added hooks to the canvas flap, so that Peter could pull it out of the way to see—or lower it to deflect arrows.

Peter had had his orders. "Tie yer hoss up at the tail o' the cart, an' climb up behind Aleck. Don't talk an' don't git in 'is way." Reluctant as he was, he knew better than to hesitate. Once up on his perch, he noticed that Aleck had his gun across his lap.

"If there's any trouble, get down on the floor and lie still."

Uncle Seth, as always, rode ahead, and five of the other men fanned out behind him, their guns also across their saddles. Their wariness increased as they neared the patch of trees. It was, of course, not possible for the wagons to ford the stream four abreast. They would have to go single file, and thus expose themselves to fire from both sides. Peter's hair stood on end—he tingled all over. To everyone's amazement nothing happened when Uncle Seth and the others reached the creek— even when they disappeared among the trees. There was not a sound. Peter held his breath. In no time at all one of the men reappeared and waved to the rest to come on.

Aleck led the way into the trees, down the slope, and into the water. The mules wanted to stop and drink their fill, but were allowed only a taste before being forced to climb up the other bank. The horsemen sat motionless, their eyes probing the shadows. As soon as the first wagon was safely across, Uncle Seth and two others rode on cautiously. Peter could tell from the sounds to the rear that the oxen drivers were having difficulties with their teams as the poor animals were determined to drink their fill. This grove, green and pretty as it was, could easily prove a death trap. They got out of it as fast as they could.

After they were again out in the open, Uncle Seth stopped short and fixed his eyes on something ahead to the left of the road. Aleck stared too, and Peter made out the burnt-out remains of a wagon, with pieces of cloth and clothing scattered about it. Then the rider's attention was attracted to something on the other side of the trail that Peter could not see. Uncle Seth stared at the ground.

"Shut your eyes, Peter," ordered Aleck. Suspecting what they were looking at, he obeyed instantly.

"Poor fools, they wuz not skeered o' Injuns!" It was Uncle Seth's voice, but Peter had never heard it sound like that.

Aleck whipped his team on again, and though his eyes were closed, Peter could tell that the mules had shied at something on the right. He heard one of the men speak:

"There's only two. What'd you reckon happened to the boy?"

"He may be layin' out there, somewheres in the woods," replied another, "or mebbe they carried him off pris'ner. If they did, I hope he didn't cry an' carry on. They mightn't've thought he was worth savin'."

"Seth, ain't you gonna bury 'em?"

"No. We're gittin' out o' here."

And on they moved.

"You c'n open your eyes now," said Aleck. "I guess you know why I made you shut 'em."

"Yes, sir."

"There's things a boy oughtn't to see. What I can't understand is why they didn't ambush us at the ford." A moment later, however, he added, "I do now. There's the reason." He pointed with his whip to a long train of covered wagons approaching slowly from the west.

"They saw they was outnumbered, and no right-thinkin' Indian wants to get caught like that."

No wonder the Comanches were overawed and kept their distance. Peter counted forty-seven wagons in the train, accompanied by many well-armed horsemen. While the train was passing, he obtained permission to resume his usual post beside Uncle Seth while Brownie scampered about, making up for the time he had lost while riding in the wagon.

One of the riders reined in his mount to allow a few words with Uncle

Seth, who told him about the killings and asked him to give the two bodies as decent a burial as was possible under the circumstances. The man agreed, and after that, the trapper seemed to feel better.

The next hours were monotonous. Even the large herds of buffalo, now that they had lost their novelty, had ceased to hold Peter's interest. But his mind was busy with other things. The discovery of the murdered men had given him a shock from which he was not to recover for a long time. The Ugly Boy, especially, was seldom absent from his thoughts. Much as he had disliked him, he wondered what had happened to him and could not help hoping that he was still alive. And the black dog? Had he ended his ill-spent days in an Indian stew-pot? Peter did think that the mules would be better off with the Indians than they had been with the men who had beaten them so badly.

They were following the almost dry bed of the Arkansas, which at this point made a great bend to the south. Uncle Seth said they were planning to camp on the far side of Ash Creek. They had neither wood nor water, so did not stop at noon. Once more it was very hot, and, to make matters worse, a very strong wind was blowing from the northwest. Peter's face was painfully burned; his dry and cracked lips ached.

But he forgot his troubles in the afternoon when Uncle Seth told him to look far ahead and see if he could see anything. Straining his eyes to the utmost, he was at last able to make out what he took to be a low hill.

"Remember Pawnee Rock I told you about in St. Louis?" As if he could ever forget it! "Wal, thet's it."

Boredom vanished at once.

"I'd love to climb it."

"You stay off it. 'Tain't safe fer grown men, let alone boys. Don't you 'member whut happened to me? Besides, we're pushin' on so's we c'n reach Ash Crik afore it turns dark."

Before they had gone many miles further, to Peter's great surprise, they met another vehicle going east. It was, he learned, a mail stage. There were three passengers inside and a cavalry escort.

"Lucky they got them soldiers."

Uncle Seth hailed one of them and reported what had happened

117

at the Walnut, including the disappearance of the Ugly Boy. The lieutenant looked very grave. "When you get to the Fort, you tell Major Chilton. Meanwhile I'll see what we can do."

"Take a good look among them bushes."

As the stage went on its way, Peter could not help wondering about the feelings of the three passengers.

When they came to Pawnee Rock, Peter's curiosity reached the bursting point. The Trail ran between it and the river, close enough to the landmark itself that he thought he could see some of the names and initials that he had been told had been cut in the soft rock. He would have given anything to carve his beside the others, but he bit his sore lips and rode silently on.

No one, however, had cautioned Brownie to watch his step, and he scooted happily about the low bushes and the small rocks which had tumbled down from the heights above. But suddenly he stopped to investigate something especially intriguing. Then he came racing back to Pluto. Peter saw that he had a small piece of blue cloth in his mouth.

"Uncle Seth! Uncle Seth!" Peter cried excitedly. "Look what Brownie has!"

Uncle Seth looked and in a jiffy was down beside the little dog. He took the cloth and examined it carefully.

"Whar's he been at?" he demanded.

"He's been running around over there among those rocks."

Uncle Seth hurried over to the cliff. "Bring him back here."

Peter dismounted, and, calling his pet, scrambled among the fallen rocks. Brownie needed no second invitation, but ran along close at his heels. Several of the other men joined them and all rummaged about in search of signs.

"Here!" called one of them, and he pointed out another blue rag caught on a cactus bush. "Are you sure that was his shirt?"

"Yes," said Peter.

"Sure looks like it," put in another.

All this time Uncle Seth had been searching the ground without speaking. "Look here!" he exclaimed, pointing to the sandy ground.

The men gathered about him.

"Thet's his footmark. Comanches don't wear shoes. Some o' them been here too," he added. "Looks like he got loose an' they cotched 'im."

"We're gonna look 'round a bit," said someone, and two of the men disappeared behind the Rock. Presently they were seen on the summit. "Nobody 'round here," one called down. When they returned, he added, "No signs at all."

Uncle Seth was squatting down, petting Brownie's head. "We'd orter do sumthin' fer this little feller."

Rising to his feet and going over to Bonita, he produced from his saddlebag a chunk of dried meat, which the hero of the occasion gulped down in short order. He seemed quite aware of his importance and to be enjoying it immensely.

"Wal, let's git movin'. No use hangin' 'round here any longer."

So much time had been lost at Pawnee Rock that it was doubtful if they could reach Ash Creek before dark, even though it was only six miles away. They were all the more anxious to get across it in daylight because of the ominous absence of buffalo, particularly because countless numbers had been grazing on both sides of the road earlier. Some of these had been shot and butchered, and pieces of meat had been hung along the sides of the wagons to dry in the scorching sun; so they could be eaten later. There didn't seem to be much grass, but the great animals evidently had found enough to satisfy their needs. The fact that they had disappeared altogether caused great alarm.

119

Peter observed that the increasing darkness was not entirely the result of the coming of night—the sun was obscured by storm clouds in the west. Uncle Seth rode back and urged the drivers to push on as fast as they could. Peter always hated to hear the loud cracking of whips that followed such an order. He still was not used to seeing animals forced to strain so hard.

10

The Pawnees Attack

Finally Ash Creek appeared, and Peter and Uncle Seth crossed the dry sandy bed without difficulty, despite the fact that on the near side the bank was steep. Then there was trouble. There was the sound of a crash. Looking back, they saw that the right rear corner of Aleck's wagon was low and the wagon stopped. With much yelling and cursing, several men took hold and managed to get it back up the slope and out of the way of the rest. Admonishing Peter to stay where he was, Uncle Seth crossed back to help with the difficult job of removing the collapsed wheel and getting the iron rim back on. The wood of the wheel had shrunk with the heat and dryness. They would have to put wedges between the iron and wood and wrestle the wheel back on the axle.

The last wagon had no more than gained the west side than the heavens opened and rain fell in torrents. This was not, however, an electrical storm like the one that had frightened Peter before. Yet in its own way, it was just as bad. The miserable little streambed which minutes before had been bone-dry was filled with rushing muddy water. As for Peter, there was nothing for him to do but sit on Pluto and get soaked to the skin. To complicate matters, darkness had fallen, and it was no easy job to maneuver the wagons into their corral formation surrounding as many animals as could be squeezed into the circle. After some time, during which Peter had sat rather bewildered on Pluto, one of the drivers called to him to get down and crawl under his wagon.

"Do you think the Indians are going to attack us?"

"Wouldn't be surprised—'bout daylight prob'ly. You just stay quiet an' keep yer head down."

The boy promptly obeyed these orders and put in an utterly wretched night. He was wet to the skin, cold, hungry, and, furthermore, was frightened about his two friends who were working on the far side of the now raging creek. His one comfort was his little dog, whom he clutched close to him. For once, he was unable to sleep, but lay on the ground, shivering with cold and fear, waiting for the war cries of the savages.

He had to wait a long time, but heard them at last, just as it was beginning to get light. They proved to be more horrible than he had imagined. Never had he heard anything so terrifying—loud yells, shrill and bloodcurdling—and they came from all directions. They were accompanied by a fusillade of shots and the whistling of arrows. Brownie struggled to his feet and let loose the most threatening barks

The Pawnees Attack

he could muster, but was promptly pulled back down under the blanket. Meanwhile the defenders replied with deadly gunfire from the rim of the corral. There was a cry of pain from a wounded ox.

To his enormous relief, Peter soon heard through the awful din a sound of splashing and crashing, followed by the voices of Uncle Seth and Aleck. He knew that, though not completely safe, they were on the right side of the creek. They drove their wagon up next to the one under which Peter lay—there was no way for them to get into the circle. The bedlam grew worse with the neighing and bawling of the terrified animals. Fortunately, the downpour had subsided into a shower.

Peter could not tell how long the attack lasted—it seemed like hours. But stop it did at last. The shots became fewer as the Indians gave up and fled.

"Peter! Peter! Whar are you?" It was Uncle Seth. At least he had not been killed.

"Here I am, under this wagon." And he emerged, dragging his blanket with him. "Is Aleck all right?"

"Right as you are. I wondered whar you wuz, but didn't have no time to look fer you."

Having made sure that Pluto was intact, Peter had another question to ask, but he could barely get it out.

"Did . . . did anybody get killed?"

"Nobody belongin' to us, but I cal'ate three or four o' them Pawnees won't never steal no more hosses er ennything else."

"Pawnees? I thought they were Comanches."

"I knowed by their yells. They're always lookin' for somethin' to steal or kidnap. But this bunch ran into more then they wuz lookin' fer, an' they hightailed it fer home. I hope they don't come back with some more an' lay fer us at Pawnee Fork. Wal, if they do we'll lick 'em agin. Now, sonny, you've ben in a real Injun fight, an' you'll hev sumthin' to tell the other boys when you git home."

Peter was glad that Uncle Seth took it for granted that he would get home again.

The fight over, everybody seemed to forget it and concentrate on getting ready to move. There was plenty of water, and the animals were allowed to drink as much as they wanted. The human beings had

122

a breakfast of sorts. Before long they were on their way with guards riding on both sides of the train on the alert for signs of more Indians. But there were none, not even at Pawnee Fork. Probably they were frightened off by the detachment of soldiers protecting a mail stage, which caught up with the slow-moving wagons as they headed for Fort Atkinson. The lieutenant was shown the piece of the shirt Brownie had found and took it to show to Major Chilton. He asked Uncle Seth why he thought the murders had been committed by Comanches and not Pawnees.

"'Cause they had leather thongs draggin' from their moccasins. I seen the marks in the sand. Thet's Comanche sign."

The next two days were a continuing ordeal for all. The clouds had disappeared and the sun beat down mercilessly. Uncle Seth had decided to use a short cut to the Fort, and so they left the river, and struggled slowly and painfully over an up-and-down sandy road. There was nothing to be seen but a dreary flatness wherever one looked. The buffalo had drunk what little water the rain had left in their wallows. But the heat and dryness had not discouraged the mosquitoes and, probably being thirsty themselves, they attacked with intensified ferocity as soon as the sun went down.

By the middle of the second afternoon, the strength had been drained out of the unfortunate oxen and there was nothing to do but stop and let them rest, hoping that the cool night would refresh them at least a little.

Shortly before daybreak one of the guards gave the alarm and pointed to a number of horsemen approaching from the west. They turned out to be, not hostile Indians, but dragoons from the Fort on a scouting expedition to try to find signs of the Ugly Boy and his captors. They had brought water for the human beings—and, Peter saw to it, for Brownie. They said they planned to cross the river into the domain of the Comanches since they seemed to have been the guilty ones. Peter always got a queer feeling in the pit of his stomach when he thought of his former enemy as a prisoner in their hands.

Because the oxen were somewhat restored, the party made a very early start in order to get as far as they could before the heat again became intense. They soon found themselves again on the banks of the Arkansas, and, though the river was very low, there was water enough for everyone.

They had a little breakfast, too, and then proceeded toward Fort Atkinson without halting at noon. It came in sight early in the evening.

This was the first real fort Peter had ever seen, though of course he had seen pictures of several. He did not know exactly what he had anticipated, but, except for its size, he found it a little disappointing. It was merely a low building made of mud and sod—there were no high towers or battlements. But it was the biggest building he had seen since leaving Independence, and, standing by itself on the bleak plain, was in its own way rather impressive. At this point the river was running more east than south, and the fort was not far from the sandy bed. He did notice that, instead of being square or rectangular like the forts he had seen in pictures, it narrowed down toward the south.

The newcomers were admitted through a gate at one corner into a sort of courtyard which, by the time they were all inside, was so crowded they could hardly move. There were many soldiers with their mounts—they had to make room for the caravan. Peter did learn by keeping his ears open that ordinarily wagons were kept outside under guard, but that because of recent events, Major Chilton had ordered all inside, no doubt a safer, but by no means more comfortable arrangement. There was much grumbling. If the Major heard any of this, he did not let on. He did not intend to risk any lives, and discomfort was not important.

As the travelers and the officers sat around the fire after supper, swatting at the swarms of vicious mosquitoes that pursued them everywhere, the discussion centered on the route the train should take on leaving the Fort in the morning. Should they, like most caravans, ford the river and strike off across the dry, barren country for the valley of the Cimarron in New Mexico, or should they keep to the right bank as far as Bent's Fort and then, after crossing to the south side, head for the mountains, struggle over "the Raton," and finally drop to the plains beyond and join the southerly road at Fort Union? The former was ordinarily preferred because it was shorter. But just now the Major and the others had their doubts. The so-called "dry route" had not been given that name without reason, and recently there had been even less rain south of the Arkansas than usual. Moreover, the dreaded Comanches had been reported to be very much in evidence of late, and a small train might prove a great temptation. Peter, sitting quietly to one side, scratching Brownie's head, was all ears. Like his elders he was torn by conflicting wishes. On the one hand, he was anxious to reach Santa Fe as soon as possible, on the other, he dreaded the stifling heat and the thirst. He was not eager to undergo another Indian attack. The mysterious fate of the Ugly Boy was seldom absent from his thoughts, and he could imagine nothing more horrible than being taken prisoner by the Comanches.

Of course, his opinion was not sought. The question was threshed over for hours, some of the men taking one side, some the other. In the end the advice of the military men prevailed—it would be the route over "the Raton." Uncle Seth had thought this would be the case since talking to the men at Council Grove. There was some muttering, but no rebellion. What they had seen at the Walnut had made too deep an impression.

Very early the next morning, Peter and his companions said goodbye to Fort Atkinson. It may not have been very imposing, but they had been treated with great hospitality, and had been given a good dinner and, what was even better, plenty of good drinks—Peter's was, of course, plain water. Major Chilton wished them well, and they were soon on their way again.

Before long Uncle Seth called Peter's attention to two holes near the right side of the road.

"Them's the Caches," he said.

"Cash?" repeated the boy. "What are they?"

"'Bout twenty-five years ago a couple o' traders who'd ought to hev known better tried to make it to Santa Fe the wrong time o' the year, got snowed in an' hed to spend the winter on thet island in the river. Most o' their stock froze to death an' when spring come along, they didn't hev enough left to haul their stuff. So they dug these holes an' buried it till they could come back fer it. Thet wuz a long time ago, an' the holes has nearly filled up, but you c'n see whar they wuz."

"But why do they call them 'the Cash'?"

"They tell me thet's the French word for hide. The ole-time trappers used it. Don't know no French myself. Right about here's the Cimarron Crossin'. Thet's the way we'd be goin' if it warn't fer the Comanches an' no water."

The next ten days did at least offer some variety. One was so fearfully hot and dry that Aleck invited Peter to join him and climb in the wagon, where at least he would be protected from the direct rays of the sun. He tied Pluto to the tail of the cart and climbed up with Brownie in his arms. The poor little animal was suffering from heat, thirst, and sore feet, but had kept up all the same. Peter thought even Mrs. Morris would be sorry for him. This arrangement was very welcome; nevertheless, Peter had an uneasy feeling that Uncle Seth did not regard it with the same enthusiasm. After that, he stayed on Pluto.

Although some days were fearfully hot, there were heavy rains in others, which complicated the fording of one or two creeks, but did supply them with all the water they wanted. There were, moreover, almost always hundreds—sometimes thousands—of buffalo in sight. So there was plenty of fresh meat and less fear of lurking Indians.

At last, to his delight, they began to see trees, good-sized ones, more than they had seen since leaving Council Grove. It had never occurred to him that he could be so glad to see trees. All his life he had taken them for granted and had rarely given one a second thought. Now these made him feel almost at home, and he stared at them as if he had never seen a tree before. They evidently had much the same effect on Brownie, who ran to them and raced into the cool shade. Peter almost called him back, but thought better of it and, instead, rode up beside Aleck.

His Scots friend obviously sensed his feelings. "Nice to see trees again—somethin' really green. Pretty soon we'll be at Bent's Fort. Then you'll see a fort that's a fort—not make-believe, like Atkinson."

He would have continued, but suddenly the quiet was shattered by the sound of excited barking coming from somewhere in the grove.

"Wonder what he's run into."

Peter was off in a flash, only to meet his pet barking madly as he ran out of the woods as fast as his short legs could carry him. But there was nothing chasing him. He rushed up to Peter and, looking excitedly up at him, continued his frantic barking. Then, still barking, he sped back toward the trees, only to stop short to be sure he was being followed.

"Little feller's seen somethin'. Best find out whut it is." Uncle Seth dismounted quickly and hurried after the barking dog.

As quickly as he could, Peter followed suit. But before he had taken

Chapter Ten

many steps, he heard Uncle Seth calling urgently "Come here, some of you. Come arunnin'!"

Pushing his way through the bushes, Peter came on him kneeling by a prostrate form that was face down in the dirt. One look was enough to tell him that it was the Ugly Boy, almost naked, his back a mass of cuts and clotted blood. Suddenly everything began to whirl about him, his legs gave way, and he sank to the ground.

Several men, Aleck the first, came up on the run.

"Is he dead?"

"No," Uncle Seth bent over him. "He's breathin'—Jest."

Very gently he turned the boy over. Opening his eyes, he gave a piercing scream, but the effort was too much for him, and he fell back, unconscious. Struggling to his feet, Peter approached the group. Brownie was cautiously sniffing the limp figure.

"Get away, Brownie. Take him, Peter."

"What he needs is a shot o' whiskey," put in one of the spectators.

"No, no, no!" exclaimed Uncle Seth. "His belly's empty. It might kill 'im. Somebody cook up a hunk o' meat, an' we'll give him a little o' the juice. Anybody got a spoon? An' hurry up. We ain't got no time to lose."

Aleck hurried back to the wagon and, after digging among his boxes, produced a spoon. One of the teamsters brought a small piece of buffalo meat and another some water. In a minute a fire was crackling, and the meat and water were dumped into a small pot. It took almost no time for the liquid to come to a boil and to begin to turn a brownish color. Taking the pot and the spoon, Aleck hurried back to Uncle Seth, who was still kneeling by the prostrate figure.

Once more the boy's head was raised. Once more his eyes fluttered open, and he started to cry out in terror.

"Easy there! Nobody's gonna hurt you. We ain't Injuns. We're yer friends. Jest try to swaller a little o' this an' you'll feel better."

Uncle Seth forced his mouth open and managed to insert the spoon and pour a little of the juice between the lips. The first mouthfuls came back up. But patiently Uncle Seth tried again and again until he got several down. As he worked, he gave instructions to the men in the circle about him.

"Let's git 'im in a wagon an' push on to the Fort as fast as we kin. It's only ten or twelve mile. Mebbe thar's a doctor thar. Some o' the rest keep yer eyes peeled. Thar ain't likely to be no Injuns this close to the Fort, but we ain't takin' no chances."

One of the drivers volunteered, "I can make room in my wagon. I'll drive it up close."

He did so in no time at all, and the emaciated body was lifted gently in among the tarpaulin-covered heaps of merchandise. There was no sound except one or two cries of pain as some sore spot was touched.

"Somebody orter ride with him, but thar ain't much room."

Uncle Seth looked over the crowded group. His eyes fell on Peter.

"Here, yer the littlest. You c'n squeeze in."

This was an arrangement Peter had not reckoned on. But protest was out of the question and in he climbed.

"What about Brownie?"

"I'll take care of him," said Aleck. "Nobody's goin' to let anything happen to him, after what he just done. I'll put him up behind me."

Peter's feelings were mixed. He had good reason for disliking the Ugly Boy—he had heard that his name was Jeff—and he had done so more intensely than he had ever disliked anyone else in his life. But this poor creature lying beside him among the bales of goods did not seem like his old enemy. He was so gaunt that he was almost unrecognizable, and his skin, where it was not covered with dried blood and dirt, was pale in spite of the sunburn. He never once opened his eyes during the whole ride. The only sounds he made were an occasional groan and a feeble cry when the wagon, rattling and bumping over the road, hit an especially rough spot. So Peter's old hostility was overwhelmed by pity and by fear that Jeff might die while they were alone together.

Looking out, he could see that they had left the rest of the plodding ox-train far behind. To his intense relief Uncle Seth and Bonita appeared without warning at the tail of the wagon.

"How's he doin'?"

"He don't say. But he's still alive. I can see him breathin'."

"Wal, if he seems worse, you holler."

After what had seemed hours, the wagon stopped, and Peter could hear voices. Then Uncle Seth and several other men gathered about the wagon. His responsibility ended, Peter was glad to jump down to earth and look about.

As no one paid any attention to him, he walked off a little way and gazed at the Fort. He saw at once that Aleck had been right; it was much more imposing than Fort Atkinson. Actually, it was no bigger, but the walls were higher and made of stone. He did not know until later that this was the New Bent's Fort, and it was still being built. It replaced the original Bent's Fort thirty miles further on, which had been destroyed in 1849 by William Bent because times had changed—trade with the Indians, who were on a rampage, had dried up, and crowds of people were rushing to California for gold. Peter would have found the old one really impressive. Trading at the new site had started a couple of years earlier in log cabins. Peter knew none of this, nor would he have cared— his thoughts were far away in Santa Fe.

An agonized cry interrupted his thoughts, and he turned back to the knot of men clustered about the tail of the wagon. They lifted the injured boy out very carefully and then carried him, moaning, through the gate. Peter followed them and found himself in a courtyard surrounded by walls still under construction. All around were openings into little rooms built inside the walls. The wounded boy was carried through one.

As Peter stared about, he was startled to see several children playing in a corner. After his curiosity had been satisfied, he walked outside again to wait for the rest of the wagon train and, most importantly, for Brownie. He had a long wait and ample opportunity to take in the surroundings. To his surprise, he found a number of Indians, both men and women, wandering about quite casually. He didn't know they were Cheyennes who had traded with William Bent for years, first at the old fort and now at this one. He was, thus, quite worried when two of the squaws approached and examined him carefully, even touching him and feeling his clothing. Some of his blonde hair stuck out from beneath the brim of his hat, and, to his great discomfort, one of the two reached out and tugged at it till he drew away. He wondered if she were about to scalp him. But she just laughed and, to his relief, they went off towards four tepees surrounded by yelping dogs.

Peter suddenly remembered the brass buttons he had cut off the blue coat in Independence and what Uncle Seth had said about trading. He pulled them from his pocket, where they somehow had managed to stay, and ran after the squaws. They were still laughing, but turned when they heard him coming and examined the glittering objects that Peter held out to them. One of them pulled out a short string of beads, which she had traded for earlier, and offered them in exchange. Peter accepted quickly. He didn't know if he had gotten a bargain, but the last remnants of the detested St. Louis outfit were now gone.

After several long hours had passed, the wagons came into sight. Sure enough Pluto was hitched to the rear of the one in the lead, and there was Brownie sitting on a box behind Aleck. As soon as he saw Peter, he became frantic with excitement and, heedless of the distance to the ground and the threat of the large wheels, leaped into the air. One would have thought they had been parted for at least a year. Peter squatted down and had his face thoroughly licked while he hugged the squirming little animal.

He later remembered the night spent at Bent's Fort vividly. First, he was given a wonderful meal—all he could stow away—including the only milk he had tasted since leaving Council Grove. He had noticed a single cow among the other animals. Nor was Brownie overlooked; in fact, he was pretty much the hero of the occasion. His little stub of a tail must have just about worn itself out, for it never stopped wagging. Yet all the time, as if fearing another separation, he stayed close to his owner.

130

"Smart dog you have there," said one of the men attached to the Fort. "Smartest in the world."

"See that cannon up there?" he inquired, pointing to the northwest corner. "Like to have a look?"

Peter needed no urging, and, with Brownie tagging along, he accompanied his new friend up the still unfinished stairs, which another man was coming down.

"Charlie," said the first man, "this is the smartest dog in the world, the one who found that poor kid down there, and this is Peter, who goes along with him. You can't have one without the other."

Charlie acknowledged the introduction, and then asked, obviously referring to Jeff, "How's he makin' out?"

"I haven't seen him, but they think he'll pull through. The women are taking care of him, feeding him a bit, washing the dirt off and dressing his wounds. He's still so weak he hasn't been able to talk. Poor kid!"

Charlie shook his head and went on across the enclosure while Peter was led to the top of the wall. He found himself beside a huge telescope pointed in the only direction from which the Fort could be approached.

"Let's find out how good a watchman you'd make. Take a squint."

Fitting his eye to the lens, Peter peered through. But it was growing dark and he could hardly see the distant tepees.

"What are those Indians doing here?" he asked.

"Come to do a little trading. But they haven't much—just a few measly pelts. You should have seen the old fort years ago. Then there were hundreds of them, and we did a big business." Peter didn't mention his small trade.

"Didn't they ever attack the Fort?"

"Knew better. Anyway, they wanted to trade. But they sometimes had fights with each other. Not many come now. Lots died of the diseases the white man brought. Beaver trade's about over. But we still keep a close watch and never let many in at the same time. And as soon as it begins to get dark, out they go."

He glanced at the blankets piled by the wall. "By the way, how'd you like to sleep up here? Got to sleep somewhere. Nobody here but me till Charlie comes back to take his turn."

"That would be wonderful—if Uncle Seth says I can."

"You go down and ask him. He probably thinks you're lost."

So down Peter went. He found Uncle Seth quickly enough, but so deeply involved in a conversation that he did not even notice his charge, and the latter knew better than to interrupt. He heard him say, "Sure, beavers is done fer, but we need the Fort."

Just then he became conscious that Aleck was staring at him, but not in his usual friendly way.

"Where's Pluto?"

Peter went cold all over. He had left his horse outside the Fort and forgotten about him entirely. To forget one's mount was, he did not need to be told, about the worst sin anybody could commit. He was scarcely able to stammer out a reply.

"Outside the . . . g-gate. I forgot him." And he looked down at his feet.

The Pawnees Attack

"How do you figger on gettin' him in? The gates are closed for the night, and do you think those Indians will leave him there till it suits you to come and get him?"

He had never heard Aleck's voice so cold and hard. The boy was overwhelmed with shame and fright. No wonder Uncle Seth had not spoken to him. It was all he could do to keep from bursting into tears.

"What'll I do?"

"Lucky for you, I found him just as one of those savages was fixing to help himself. So he's back in the corral eating his head off. Your gear's over there by the wall."

His relief was so great that again he had to fight back the tears. "I was just so excited I forgot. What'll Uncle Seth do to me?"

"He'd do plenty—if he knew. But he don't know, and nobody's going to tell him. So just keep your mouth shut." Knowing that Peter had learned his lesson, he put his hand on the boy's shoulder. "I know it'll never happen again."

"No, sir!" Then, as Aleck started to turn away, he remembered what he had come to find out. "A man wants me to sleep up on the wall." He pointed to it. "I came down to ask Uncle Seth if it would be all right. But he's busy."

"I'll tell him where you are. And, Pete, don't stay awake all night cryin' over spilt milk."

When he had mounted the wall again, he was in no mood to ask his host the questions he had planned to put to him, but got himself to bed, with Brownie at his feet, and wrestled silently with his guilty conscience. The realization that he had neglected to thank Aleck for all he had done for him did not help any. But even his remorse could not keep him awake long.

The next thing he knew, Charlie was shaking him, greatly to the displeasure of Brownie, who contented himself with fierce growls. It was still dark, and Peter could see little about him.

"You sure slept sound. Shut up, Brownie," said the man. "Now you better get yourself downstairs in a hurry or Seth'll be climbin' them steps to find out what's happened to you. He wants to git under way early."

This time Peter did remember to say thank you, and having gathered up his bedding, he stumbled down to the patio. It was already filled with the

Chapter Ten

light from many lanterns. Men worked everywhere. He found Uncle Seth and a bit nervously presented himself for duty. To his great relief, the old trapper evidently knew nothing about his recent crime, for his greeting was hearty. He ordered him to eat some breakfast at once and get ready to start. Peter gobbled down the best breakfast he had enjoyed in weeks, saddled Pluto, and was waiting outside the gate when Uncle Seth and Aleck emerged.

The company was quickly lined up in its usual formation and on its way along the north bank of the Arkansas. Eager to atone for at least one of his sins, he reined Pluto in alongside Aleck. For a moment he was afraid to say anything; then, having made sure that Uncle Seth was not within earshot, he murmured, "Thanks for taking care of Pluto last night."

"Let's ferget aboot last night. Everybody makes mistakes sometimes, and it won't happen again."

"No, sir," said Peter fervently; then, after a pause, "How's Jeff?"

"He's better. The women are takin' good care of him. He'll get well after a while."

"Did he say what happened to him?"

"He's still too weak to do much talkin'. But I'm told he did say that, after those Comanches killed the two men, they tied him to a horse and carried him off. They didn't treat him very bad till he ran away there near Pawnee Rock. When they caught him, they beat him somethin' terrible. Kept him tied up and didn't give him hardly anything to eat or drink."

"How'd he get away?"

"One night they run into a passel of other Indians, Pawnees prob'ly, since it was this side of the river. They had a big fight, and in the darkness he got loose again and hid out in the trees till Brownie smelt him out."

"If he'd shot Brownie that time, he'd be dead himself now."

"That's right."

Peter never heard another word of the Ugly Boy—he was not sorry.

133

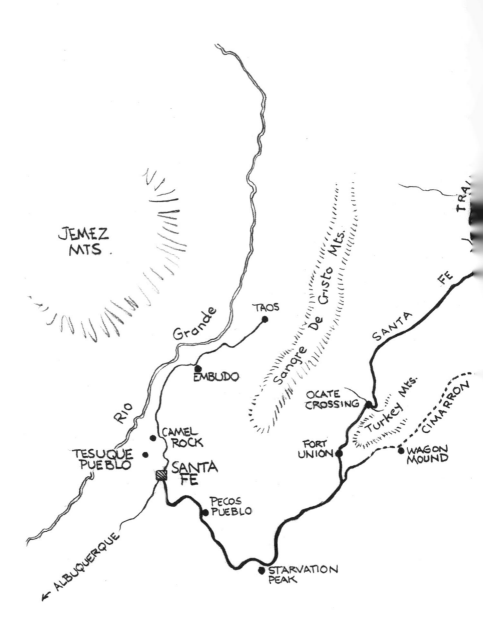

Arkansas

BENT'S
OLD FORT

BENT'S
NEW FORT

River

FORT ROUTE

Purgatoire River

ON

CKS

ROUTE

Santa Fe Trail

1" = 25 miles

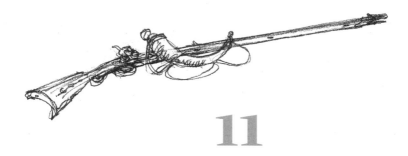

11

A Grizzly Threatens

After they had covered close to twenty miles, they turned south to the river, and Uncle Seth rode Bonita into the water and headed for the other side. He ordered Peter to take Brownie up into the saddle and keep close behind him. The river, though fairly wide, was so shallow that they did not even wet their shoes. Once across, they reined their horses in and watched the first two wagons till they were on dry land. Not till then did the old man start on.

"Hev to be on the lookout fer quicksand," observed Uncle Seth.

"Quicksand? What's that?"

"I dunno what it is, but I do know it's bad. Thar's patches of it at the bottom o' the Arkansas. Jest sucks anythin' that steps on it down out o' sight an' nuthin' left to show fer it. Last year I seen a mule git hisself swallered up, pack'n all. Couldn't do nuthin' to save him. He jest sunk down'n down till thar warn't nuthin' left to see. Sometimes same thing happens to whole wagons. So gotta be keerful. This ford's all right, though—thar ain't none here. Better fill yerself up with water—Pluto'n Brownie too. An' don't fergit yer canteen. We ain't likely to see no more water fer quite a spell."

Peter dismounted and obeyed instructions. As for the two animals, they did not need any instructions except those Nature gave them.

"Let's git a move on," cried Uncle Seth.

Turning their backs on the river, they set off toward the southwest. The country was very different from the level plain they had traveled across for so long. It was rolling, and they threaded their way among low sand hills. A hot wind was blowing and so was the sand. Peter wished it were all at the bottom of the Arkansas. It covered everything in sight, making the little bushes that managed to live here and there look gray. Worse still, it coated the men's faces, filled their ears, and made their eyes sting. Poor little Brownie was in such obvious distress that his master put him in front on the saddle and covered everything but his black nose with his coat. Their discomfort was made even worse by the sun, which, the higher it rose, the more cruelly it beat down on them. Peter's mouth was full of sand, and his fingers were so gritty that it was hard to wipe his eyes.

Between gusts of wind, Uncle Seth treated Peter to a lesson in history. "Up to a few years ago all this here country wuz part o' Mexico. But Gen'ral Kearny tuk it from 'em, and now it's part o' the United States—sand, rattlers, Injuns, an' all."

"Why did he take it?"

"The President told him to. It wuzn't doin' them Mexicans no pertickler good—an', besides, we wanted it. So he tuk it."

"If it belonged to the Mexicans, didn't they fight for it?"

"No, they jest turned tail an' run. Besides, the Governor wuz sort o' hard up fer cash. They say we giv' it to him. I dunno 'bout thet, but, anyhow, he found out he had important bizness down the Rio Grande, an' he made tracks along with his army an' all the valuables he could lay his hands on."

"He can't have been very patriotic."

The old timer snorted so loud he made Pluto jump. "He wuz patriotic fer himself. You'll see the palace he used to live in in Santa Fe. American guvnor in it now. By the way, they say he come from St. Louis. Mebbe you know him."

"What's his name?"

"Thet's all I know. Don't ask me no more questions."

Peter rode on in silence. There were many, many questions jumping about in his mind—but no answers—and still the fear that Pa had gone off somewhere.

By mid-afternoon the oxen were in such a bad way that Uncle

Seth halted the train until dark. The drivers of ox teams did not ride, but walked by the left lead animal—they did not question the decision to stop. Aleck had again enticed the boy and the dog up behind him to give them a little relief from the direct rays of the sun. Uncle Seth saw, but if he had any objections, he kept them to himself. The moment the sun went down, it grew cooler; so they resumed their march slowly and, for the animals, painfully. Every man and beast was suffering from thirst, but at least they were not being roasted alive. Some time after dark one of the teamsters reported that he had found a couple of pools with a little water in them. There was not much, and Peter thought it tasted sickeningly bad, but at least everybody got a sip. After he had swallowed his mouthful, he was able to choke down a few bites of dried meat and then felt better. After a rest of two hours they pushed on. The trail changed—they were steadily going up, and the sand was not so deep.

The next day was not so bad. The ground became firmer and firmer. It was rockier—large boulders were all about them. The trees were taller and not gray with dust. What's more, he could see mountains in the distance. That night there were two rain showers—men and animals felt better.

Peter thought it took forever to reach the mountains, but at last they did. A good-sized river flowed from their midst. The water was clear and cool, not warm and gritty like that in the Arkansas. Uncle Seth called it the "Picketwire," but Aleck argued that its right name was the "Purgatorie." This disagreement left Peter none the wiser, for he did not know what either name meant. He was relieved to learn that, whatever the name was, they were going to stop and rest for a whole day on the grass under the trees that grew beside the water.

He would later realize that this rest was needed before they tackled "the Raton," which loomed above them to the south. It made a formidable barrier across their path, one enormous rock piled on top of another, surmounted by a huge square boulder that reminded him of Aleck's wagon. He hated to lose a day, but it was a treat to lie on the cool grass and watch Brownie scout about enthusiastically as if he had never known the hardships of the Trail.

Chapter Eleven

It took the party six days to get over the "pass." There was nothing that even suggested a road, and the heavy, ponderous wagons had to be pulled and pushed up steep inclines and over great stones that blocked their path. Sometimes it took half a dozen men to hold them and keep them from crashing down into empty streambeds and smashing to pieces. The mules and the oxen tugged and strained; the men pushed with all the strength they had and filled the air with curses. The wagons creaked and groaned. Wheels flew off and tongues broke. Repairing them was slow. They did well to make three or four miles a day. Tempers flared, and fights were narrowly averted.

Peter was a bit ashamed, because he was really enjoying himself. Exhilarated by the high, cool mountain air, he felt a new surge of strength. He felt there was nothing he could not do. So he tried to lend a hand with the wagons, only to be chased off by Aleck, who told him that it was man's work and a boy like him would only get hurt. His pride was hurt, but his conscience was clear, and he felt free to indulge in a little exploration. So when it was obvious that a long halt was certain, he tied Pluto to a tree, and with Brownie in tow started to scramble over the rocks to see what he could see. However, when Uncle Seth became aware of these activities, they stopped instantly.

"These here mountains is full o' varmints—bars, painters, an' wolves, an' mebbe an Injun or two. You might git hurt. It's no place fer a boy to go scoutin' around on his own. So you stick close to the road, an' keep Brownie close to you. Mind whut I say."

"Yes, sir," Peter answered obediently.

He could not see anything that even remotely resembled a road, but he knew what Uncle Seth meant, and did what he was told. On the other hand, Brownie had not understood the instructions and was even more excited. There were so many wonderful sights and smells, especially smells, that there was no stopping him. For the first time in his short life he disobeyed the shrill commands of his owner.

One afternoon, having ignored the rules, he took off on a journey of exploration through the rocks and the pine trees. But it was not destined to be a long trip. He had not been out of sight five minutes when Peter was alarmed by the sound of frenzied barking, and he was about to ignore

*. . . the furious bear found himself confronted
by an array of wagons, men, and animals . . .*

his orders and set off on a rescue expedition when in a flash of brown the little dog came tearing like mad out from the trees, and headed straight for the safest spot he knew, his master's arms. Close behind him was a bear bigger than Peter could have imagined, not a black or cinnamon-colored one, but an enormous gray-brown beast, altogether a terrifying brute. It was lucky for boy and dog that they did not have to face him alone. If they had, their journey would have ended on "the Raton."

But when the furious bear found himself confronted by an array of wagons, men, and animals, he abruptly applied his brakes and slid to a dead stop. Instead of charging on, he rose up on his hind legs and took stock of the situation before deciding what to do next.

He was not the only one surprised. The whole wagon train was thrown into a panic. Horses and mules reared up on their hind legs, oxen bellowed and struggled to break loose from their traces. Men yelled and hung on to their animals. Peter gathered up his terrified pet and clutched him tight to his chest.

"Lemme git my gun," yelled one of the drivers. "I'll fix him!"

"Put thet gun down!" roared Uncle Seth. "Ever'body jest stand still. Don't you move."

All the men, except those hanging on to the terrified animals, stood as if frozen. After what seemed hours, the huge animal dropped to all fours and went back into the woods from where he had come. Everyone breathed again. But Uncle Seth had too much stifled rage to relax. He had to take it out on someone. That someone was Peter.

He charged down on him, his eyes blazing. "Didn't I tell you to stay here?" he demanded furiously.

"I did. I stayed right here."

Man and boy confronted each other.

"Thet dog o' yourn then. He like to hev got some of us kilt. I could kill him!"

Peter stood motionless, paralyzed with fear, but he stared up at the man, and held his dog tight to his bosom. "Don't you hurt Brownie!"

"Take it easy, Seth." It was Aleck, coming to the rescue again. Uncle Seth whirled on him, but his partner stood his ground. "Nobody's done anythin' wrong. It's natural fer a dog to run about. Pete couldn't stop him."

A Grizzly Threatens

Uncle Seth's rage began to subside, but he was not through yet. "Alf, you jest about got us all kilt, callin' fer yer gun an' wantin' to shoot. You gotta hit one o' them bars square a'tween the eyes. You couldn't hit a mountain ef you wuz standin' on it! We'd a had eight hundred pounds of wounded grizzly tearin' us to pieces!"

Having got this off his chest, he felt better, and after a moment slowly turned back to Peter. "I ain't gonna hurt Brownie. You know thet." He reached down and gave the little dog a pat on the head. "I'm sorry I lost my temper. But I wuz skeered near out o' my britches. Grizzlies is the most dangerous varmints in these here mountains, an' a wounded one is all Hell bust loose. Don't let it happen agin."

"I'll try. You think he's gone?"

"He ain't gone very fur, but he thought thar wuz too many of us to take on. Keep yer eyes open, an' you an' Brownie stay close like I told you."

Then he turned back to business, which meant getting the train started again. The animals had recovered from the worst of their panic, and in a moment or two order had been restored.

Peter was not really good at controlling Brownie's zest for exploration most of the time. Now, however, the little dog had lost all of his interest in adventure. He had learned a lesson, which he remembered for the time being. He could sense the great bear and did not wander far afield.

142   Yet it was too much to expect him to hold the thought for very long. The next evening, when the men were sitting about the fire, smoking, and swapping tall tales, there was the sound of a scuffle in the bushes beyond the circle of firelight. Before Peter knew what was happening, his pet came trotting out of the shadows carrying a tremendous brown rat, which he triumphantly deposited at his master's feet.

"So he's caught him a pack rat," laughed Aleck. "Guess he thought he ought to 'cause these mountains are named for them. Good dog!"

"Raton is a Spanish word fer these things. They're jest about the biggest thieves in the world. Throw it away, Pete—fur as you kin. We don't want him stinkin' up the camp." Uncle Seth was not angry now, just laughing.

Peter hurled it as far as he could. Brownie started after it, but obeyed a very stern command to stay put. So much for the raton.

This would be the last night spent in the mountains. Peter was sorry, for he had enjoyed the feeling of being surrounded by them; on the other hand, when he thought of the grizzly and Brownie's narrow escape—to say nothing of the danger to the whole company—his regret was tempered. But he was not through with "the Raton" yet. He was in for one more shock.

The nights were bitter cold, and when he went to bed, he was careful to tuck Brownie in with him under the blankets. Snuggled down close together, both kept each other warm and usually slept soundly until daylight when the noises made by the men stirring about woke them up. Not even the occasional howling of a wolf disturbed him, for by this time it was a familiar sound. But this last night was different. Suddenly the silence was broken by a new bloodcurdling sound. Peter had not heard anything like it before—worse than Pawnees. It woke him completely, and he sat bolt upright, every hair standing on end under his now battered hat. Brownie did not dare do more than growl under his breath, as it were. They both sat up frozen with horror, wondering what would happen next.

They did not have to wait long. The fearsome sound was repeated. It was a piercing scream like that of a terrified woman. Peter waited for the others to spring up and rush off to the rescue. He was about to cry out when a sleepy voice called, "Oh shut up, you!" Shivering, he lay down again and waited, hardly daring to breathe, for another to come, but none did, and in a few minutes he was once more dead to the world.

In the morning he was somewhat let down when he found no one could remember the frightful scream. Aleck said casually, "It must have been a panther." And that was that.

For the past two days the trail had gradually descended from its highest point, but had not, except in rare spots, become any smoother. Sometimes it was nothing but a rocky streambed that had to be abandoned when there was a heavy rain. Peter was sure that, if he climbed the heights that shut it in, he could enjoy wide views, but orders had to be followed, and he resisted the temptation. Besides, he did not want Brownie to go on any more bear hunts.

On the last day, however, they came to a point from which they could look out between the precipices and see a vast level plain lined on both sides by mountains and strangely shaped hills he soon learned to call mesas.

Uncle Seth called him to his side and, waving one of his great hands, said: "Wal, Peter, thar's New Mexico. What do you think of it?"

Peter did not know what he thought; so he just asked, "Where's Santa Fe?"

Uncle Seth nodded toward the southwest. "Over theta way—'bout two hundred miles. You talk as if it wuz so close we c'd see it."

"How long will it take us to get there?"

"Ten days or two weeks." He started to add, "Whut's yer hurry?," but he knew the answer to that question and stopped. "Keep yer pants on. We'll git thar. I'm makin' the best time I kin. I can't make no better."

"I know, sir. I just get sort o' worried sometimes."

"I understand, but your worryin' ain't gonna make them oxen move any faster. They're doin' the best they kin."

He pointed further to the north. "Taos is over theta way. It's a Mexican town, with an Injun pueblo thrown in. Made a sight o' trouble a few years back. But ever'thin's quiet now."

After a last day spent crashing and banging over stones as big as any they had encountered higher up, the train finally emerged from "the Raton" shortly after dark. Everyone, whether he said so or not, was overjoyed, and badly frayed tempers subsided into good humor. Nevertheless, they very shortly were faced with an encounter they had not reckoned on. To their unconcealed chagrin, they found the campsite they had counted on using already occupied by five wagons. What was worse, these wagons were drawn up in the same formation that had been the rule on the Indian-infested plains the other side of the pass.

Uncle Seth immediately set out to learn the reason. Most of the teamsters were Mexicans, and he found them very uneasy. There were only five wagons and not more than a dozen men. He learned from one who could speak passable English that a few miles back on the trail they had been threatened by a small band of Comanches, who had, however, been frightened off by a company of dragoons from Fort Union on a scouting expedition. Nevertheless, they were justifiably nervous and welcomed any addition to their numbers.

The two parties pitched their camps near each other, but there was no mixing. A watchful guard was kept all night, but no Indians appeared, and the two groups separated early in the morning—the Mexicans, obviously still frightened, plunged into the vastnesses of "the Raton," while the Americans headed off over the flat plains for Fort Union.

Travel was not as bad as it had been the other side of "the Raton." True, when the sun was out, it was scorching, but the instant it went behind a cloud, the temperature dropped. Luckily, frequent rains kept down the dust and spared both human beings and animals the distress of thirst. There was now a road made by hundreds of wagons, which had left deep ruts in the soil. It was neither sandy nor rocky, and the oxen made much better time. Peter missed the buffalo, but there were none to be seen, for there was nothing for them to eat. Almost the only forms of vegetation were low grayish sagebrush bushes and scattered clumps of prickly pear, which Peter thought were inedible. He later learned that was not true.

Once Aleck thought he spied two or three Comanches in the distance, but, if he did, they did not venture close. Nevertheless, they took no chances, and the usual guards were posted every night. One night they camped at Ocate Crossing, a ford through a small stream. Peter could just make out on the horizon to the southeast a high mesa shaped like a covered wagon. Aleck said it was called "Wagon Mound." The guards were cautioned to be especially alert. When asked why, Aleck said briefly that a few years ago Utes and Apaches had massacred the passengers of a stagecoach near its foot. When pressed for details, he shut up tight, and left Peter wondering what had happened that he was not supposed to know about.

12

"You Ain't Got a Chance"

Peter had heard people talking about Fort Union and gathered that all the wagons would spend a night there. With Bent's Fort fresh in his mind, he couldn't wait to see another new fort. Sure enough, about noon on the day after they had camped at the Ocate Crossing, they pulled up at this frontier outpost. Bent's Fort made Peter think all forts were made of stone and impressive, but this one at the base of a ridge at the edge of a vast expanse was not in the same class. Uncle Seth pointed out some mountains to the east, "They's full o' wild turkeys—call 'em the Turkey Mountains." At first Peter thought the fort consisted of nothing but a collection of dismal, unattractive log buildings, but by the time they had reached it, he saw that there were a few corrals of sorts for the horses and other animals. The whole establishment struck him as pretty forlorn.

When they dismounted—all except Uncle Seth—a number of soldiers gathered around and began firing questions at them. Then to his astonishment Peter noticed a young lady walking nearby. He had seen nobody like her since leaving St. Louis. She would not have been out of place on Fourth Street—for she wore a pretty, brightly colored dress and, of all things in this wild place, was carrying a parasol. Pausing briefly to glance at the newcomers, she spotted him, and came over for a closer inspection. The men standing about made way for her with considerable respect.

After one quick look, she came to the point at once.

"Oh, my goodness! Who are you?"

"Peter Blair, ma'am."

"What under the sun are you doing in this lonely part of the world?"

"I'm goin' to find my Pa in Santa Fe."

"Well, I'm Mrs. Bowen. My husband, Captain Bowen, is stationed here."

"Bowen!" said Peter in amazement. "My—my friend is named Bowen, too." And he indicated Uncle Seth, who was slumped on Bonita's back.

"Is that so?" She diverted her gaze momentarily to her "relative."

"Yes, ma'am," he replied, removing his weather-stained hat in a courtly gesture, "Seth Bowen. At yer service."

"We must be kin. Bowen is not a common name."

"I'm afeared not, ma'am. I ain't got no kinfolk left. All dead and planted." And he restored his hat to its proper place.

This point settled, the young lady resumed her inspection of Peter, who, with all eyes fixed on him, was beginning to feel like a public character. By this time he had followed Uncle Seth's courteous example and removed his hat.

"Oh, my goodness!" she exclaimed again on taking a second look. "How old are you?"

"Twelve, ma'am."

"Well, right now you're coming with me to my house."

Peter looked at Uncle Seth, who said: "He's got to look after his hoss."

She brushed this answer aside. "Right now he's got something more important to do. Alf," she addressed a soldier standing rather sheepishly by, "you attend to this boy's horse. Then come to my house. We've got work to do."

Uncle Seth showed signs of being about to interfere, but his protest died before it was made. Uncle Seth had met his match at last. And he knew it.

"Where are your clean clothes, Peter?"

"In my saddle-bag, ma'am." He did not add that they had been there undisturbed ever since he had left Independence.

"Get them and come with me." She took another look. "Oh, my goodness!"

She did not come right out and say that he was dirty, but he knew what she meant when she said, "Oh, my goodness!" and she said it practically every time she looked in his direction. What was more, he knew that everybody else knew too.

Without further ado, she started, parasol and all, to walk toward her house, Peter following behind her with his head down.

"You ain't got a chance," whispered one of the men as he passed him.

But Peter did not follow her alone. Brownie was tagging along.

Mrs. Bowen stopped and looked down at him. "Is that your dog?"

"Yes, ma'am."

"What's his name?"

"Brownie."

"Looks more yellow to me," she remarked after a good inspection. "But Yellow wouldn't make a nice name. Well, I know what he needs too. Come along, Brownie."

He needed no invitation. He was on his way already. Mrs. Bowen led them across a wide bare space and to one of the log houses facing it. There she paused, and, after looking down at her canine guest, told the two of them to wait and disappeared indoors. In a few minutes she was back, carrying an enormous bone for Brownie. She bestowed it on him, and he trotted off a short distance and went to work. Then she led Peter inside.

"This is our home," she told him. "And this," she added, indicating a dark-skinned woman who was dusting the nicest looking furniture he had seen since leaving Mrs. Morris's living room, "is Maria. Maria, this is Peter. Get the tub and put lots of water on the stove—and when I say 'lots,' I mean lots."

The outraged veteran of the Trail had the horrible thought that he was about to be given a bath by two women, but he knew very well that the soldier was right when he said he hadn't a chance. His hostess wasted no time waiting for the tub and the water, but, having spread a sheet about a chair, she ordered him to sit down. When he was in place, another sheet was fastened about his neck and arranged over the rest of him.

"You can't possibly go to meet your father looking like this."

She took out a formidable looking pair of scissors from a drawer in a cupboard and went to work. Snip! Snip! The sheets were soon covered with shorn locks. Peter thought of Mrs. Morris and remembered how cross

Chapter Twelve

she had always been when cutting hair. Mrs. Bowen was not cross at all.

"What color is your hair supposed to be?" she inquired.

"Blond, ma'am."

"We'll soon find out."

By the time the operation was completed, Maria had lugged in a large tin tub and a pitcher of water.

"Now kneel down and put your head over the tub."

No sooner was he in the required position than his head was doused with hot water and then lathered generously with laundry soap. Mrs. Bowen's hands may have been delicate looking, but they were astonishingly strong— and she rubbed vigorously, so vigorously, especially when she used a stiff brush, that, if her victim had not been ashamed to, he would have cried out.

A second pitcher was emptied on his head, and the tub was soon half full of brown water.

"I never saw so much dust and sand on a human head in all my born days. I don't think you left any on the Trail."

At last it was over, and what hair was left where Nature had grown it, was violently rubbed with a bath towel. Just then, to Peter's great relief, Alf appeared and he and the silent Maria staggered out of the room with the tub, only to return shortly with it full of clean water. The ordeal was by no means over.

"Now take off everything but your underwear. And get a clean set." He pulled the beads he had traded for and Father Donahue's watch from his pocket—he had forgotten to wind it. The exact time of day hadn't meant much on the Trail, but he thought it would in Santa Fe.

She gazed at him in horror. "Oh, my goodness! How long have you had those on?"

"Since we left Independence."

"Why didn't you change them?" Under the circumstances this was not an unnatural question.

"I didn't have a chance, ma'am."

"These will have to be burned. Come, Maria, it's time for you and me to retire from the scene. Alf, when he takes them off, you hand them through the door."

As soon as the two women had departed, Peter peeled off the offending and it must be confessed, offensive, union suit. Alf took care of it as directed. The boy could not help feeling that it was a little highhanded of Mrs. Bowen to burn his clothes without so much as a "by your leave," but he knew that she had justification and that he wouldn't have a chance. So he stepped into the hot water and soaped himself from head to toe. Alf poured hot water over him. They repeated the process three times and had another tub full of brown water. He didn't usually enjoy a bath, but he did this one.

He still had something else on his mind and decided to appeal to Alf for an explanation.

"What happened at Wagon Mound when the Indians attacked the stagecoach? Did they kill all the passengers?"

Alf was quite ready to oblige. "Everyone before they got through. Worse'n that, the year before, at Point of Rocks about a hundred miles before Wagon Mound, Apaches attacked a stage and killed everybody 'cept a girl, her mother, and her nurse. They carried them off an' killed the mother later. Nobody has heard a thing about the other two since. Probably traded them as slaves."

So that was why Aleck had said so little. Peter was a long time forgetting that little girl and wondering what had become of her. He never found out.

After he dried himself and put on his clean underwear, he felt like a different person. Mrs. Bowen's methods might have been a bit highhanded, but the results she got were very good.

The moment he was decently clothed, she and Maria returned to the scene of action with his outer garments.

After surveying him critically, she exclaimed, "That's more like it. Now your father will recognize you, and he won't be ashamed to introduce you to his friends."

Just at this moment an officer entered through the front door.

"Whose dog is that trying to get outside a bone that's as big as he is? I thought he wasn't going to let me in my own house."

"He's Peter's," Mrs. Bowen explained. "His name is Brownie, and he is a very nice dog. He thought you wanted to steal his bone. This is our houseguest, Peter—what did you say your last name was?"

"Blair, ma'am."

Chapter Twelve

"He's going to Santa Fe to meet his father. Only, we had a little work to do before we sent him on his way."

"I understand," replied the Captain, eyeing the tub and its brown contents being removed from the room and giving Peter an understanding wink. "How do you do, Peter? You seem to have survived my wife's heroic treatment." And he shook hands with military formality.

"He is going to have dinner with us and then spend the night."

Inasmuch as he had not been consulted, this was news to the "houseguest," but he had learned not to be surprised by anything his hostess said or did.

"My husband will tell you that I'm a pretty good cook."

"Can I go tell Uncle Seth? He's probably wondering what's happened to me."

"Don't you worry. He knows already. Alf told him."

"You see, Peter. Everything's been attended to." And the Captain permitted himself another wink. "I've learned not to worry. That's why I'm so fat and sassy. So just make yourself at home and take it easy."

"Stop putting notions into the boy's head. You two just settle down and have a good chat while Maria and I get dinner. The poor boy's half-starved."

As they had been instructed, Peter and the Captain had a "nice chat" during the course of which pretty nearly the whole of the former's life-story, especially during the past months, including his worry about finding his father still in Santa Fe, came out.

As for the dinner that followed, Mrs. Bowen had been quite right— ham and eggs, hot biscuits, fried potatoes, and, as a climax, a huge piece of apple pie—all washed down by two full glasses of cool milk. When he had eaten it all, he was so full he could hardly move and also nearly overcome with sleep. The Captain advised him to get into bed as soon as he could. Of course, he first had to check on Brownie. The latter, having almost completely demolished his precious bone, was in the land of dreams. After being rudely awakened, he managed to get to his feet and follow his master indoors. Both were so sleepy that they could scarcely walk straight.

The Captain guided them to a small bedroom, and in no time at all

Peter had crawled in between a pair of white sheets. Until he came into the Bowen household he had almost forgotten that there were such luxuries. How good they felt! It was too bad he could not stay awake to enjoy them. But that was not to be, and the next thing he knew, he was being awakened by his host, despite the growls coming from his faithful protector. He climbed out of bed, rubbing his eyes and trying to figure out where he was.

After he had made away with a big breakfast and dutifully thanked Mrs. Bowen for all she had done for him, he set out, accompanied by Brownie, to locate Uncle Seth. He was very self-conscious, not to say embarrassed—he was so clean he was ashamed—though deep down he really felt better. He had learned that Mrs. Bowen's name was "Kitty"—he thought that pretty and quite appropriate.

He found, however, that everybody was too preoccupied with more important things to notice his almost indecent cleanliness. There was trouble. He was aware of that right away. Three of the wagons had succumbed to damages suffered on the Raton, and would have to lay over a day or maybe two for repairs. As bad luck would have it, one of them was Aleck's. And if that were not trouble enough, it was obvious that Uncle Seth was sick. When Peter said good morning, he just grunted and grimaced with pain. Somebody had brought a chair. He felt so bad that even his pride could not keep him from accepting the chance to be seated—a picture of frustration.

The sight of Uncle Seth and the delay in getting to Santa Fe was too much for Peter. He was sure his father would be gone. All he could do was walk off by himself. Not even Brownie was with him, for he was scampering happily about on his own business. Peter brightened when he saw the pretty young lady carrying a blue parasol and making her morning tour of inspection. By this time she had inspired such confidence in him that he believed she could solve any problem presented to her. He hurried over and poured his woes into her sympathetic ears.

She immediately set about dealing with his problem, and he breathed more easily. But the first object of her concern was Uncle Seth. That independent old codger tried to repulse her onslaught, but, as anybody who had seen her in action before could have told him, he was beaten before he started to defend himself. She sent a soldier for the post surgeon.

Chapter Twelve

Next she tackled her husband and told him, without any ifs or buts, that Peter must be sent on to Santa Fe at once. He replied that that was out of the question, because there was no one to take him. But he added that a dozen dragoons were going to the capital after supplies the next day.

"Why can't they go today?" she demanded.

"Orders are for them to go tomorrow."

"Who issued those orders?" Her voice was sweetness itself.

"I did, of course. The Major's away."

She and he had walked a little apart from the men gathered about the wagons; so their conversation would be confidential. But in that high altitude sounds carried far, and Peter could hear almost every word.

"Is there any good reason why they can't go one day early?" she inquired sweetly.

"Orders," he answered firmly. "What would the Colonel say if he heard that military orders were changed just to suit the convenience of a twelve-year-old boy?"

"The Colonel is in Albuquerque, and what he doesn't know won't hurt him. You know perfectly well, dearest, that I wouldn't dream of asking you to do this if there were a good reason why you shouldn't. If you don't know that, you must have a very poor opinion of me." She seemed to be hurt.

"You know I have a good opinion of you." His tone was just a little brusque.

She, however, was not about to surrender, and Peter recalled again the soldier's "You ain't got a chance." Neither, he suspected and hoped, did the Captain.

"This poor boy has come all the way from St. Louis to find his father. Think how you'll feel if, just because you were so stubborn, he reaches Santa Fe only to find his father just gone! You'd never forgive yourself."

"It's late to make a start." Peter knew that the Captain was right, but the battle was over, and the victor rewarded her lord with a kiss on the cheek.

Captain Bowen started back toward the wagons. Peter was about to follow him, but Mrs. Bowen put her finger on her lips and motioned for him to stay where he was. Just as the Captain went off to issue the necessary orders, the doctor showed up and began to talk to Uncle Seth, who gave no evidence of appreciating the attention.

"You Ain't Got a Chance"

"Just a bad case of rheumatism" was the diagnosis, "nothing serious. But you'll have to take it easy for a few days."

His unwilling patient fired up. "Take it easy!" he snorted. "I promised to take this here boy to Santa Fe to find his pa, an' I ain't gonna quit. When I promise to do sumthin', I do it!"

"All right," replied the doctor. "Let's see you get on a horse." And he left, but looked over his shoulder as he walked away.

In a surprisingly short time Captain Bowen was back—followed in a few minutes by twelve mounted dragoons and a rickety looking wagon pulled by two mules. Right behind them came Aleck leading Bonita. Uncle Seth struggled to his feet with great effort and dragged himself painfully over to his pony. Peter longed to protest, but he knew enough to hold his tongue. No protest was needed, however, for that was as far as the old man got. He just stood there motionless, whipped and humiliated, with Aleck standing sympathetically beside him. After what seemed to Peter an endless period of time, he managed to speak.

"Peter, I'm lettin' you down, the first person I ever let down in my life—and you of all people. This ole carcass ain't no good any more. Tell yer pa I done my best, but I . . . ." He paused for a moment. "Tell him he's got a good boy, a boy he kin be proud of."

The boy had such a big lump in his throat that he could scarcely choke out his thanks. He turned away to hide the tears that were welling up in his eyes.

"If your father isn't there," Aleck volunteered, "Sol Spiegelberg will look after you till we get there in two or three days."

The reminder of that appalling possibility was almost more than Peter could bear, but he felt that he was on his own now and it was up to him to show what kind of stuff he was made of. He must not let Uncle Seth down—nor "Pa." So he hid his terror and said stoutly, "I'll be all right."

Mrs. Bowen put in her oar. "If you get into any sort of trouble, just go to Governor Lane. He's from St. Louis too, and he'll be a good friend."

The Captain led him to a fine looking young officer who was waiting nearby on his horse. "This is Lieutenant Clark. Lieutenant, this is Peter Blair. You two take good care of each other, and there'll be no trouble."

Chapter Twelve

"And don't you worry about Mr. Bowen. He's my charge from now on. In spite of what he says, I'm sure we must be kin." Peter was now completely convinced she could solve any problem.

At this point Alf came up, leading Pluto saddled, bridled, and ready to go. Without another word Peter climbed into the saddle.

"What are you going to do with your dog?" inquired the Captain. "You'd better leave him here with us."

"Oh no, sir!" cried out Peter, horrified by the unthinkable suggestion. "He runs along."

"Not with these horses, he won't. They will be too fast for him. If you want to take him, he'll have to ride in the wagon."

"I'll take him up here in the saddle with me. He's used to that."

This arrangement was not what Brownie had in mind, but he limited his objections to a little squirming when Aleck hoisted him up in front of his master.

"Goodbye!" Peter managed to call as they rode off. Looking back, he saw Mrs. Bowen bending solicitously over her "kin."

He was off on the last leg of his long journey from the Mississippi to the Rio Grande.

13

Santa Fe—At Last

"Well," said Lieutenant Clark as they jogged along side-by-side, "This is the home stretch for you."

Peter had no idea what a "home stretch" was, but he assumed that the Lieutenant did and that he knew what he was talking about. Whatever it was, this home stretch did not include any adventures.

"Aren't there any Indians around here?"

"Plenty of 'em—all kinds," replied the officer, glancing up at the mountains which lined both sides of the road. "But they know better than to make any trouble, at least in the daytime. Too many soldiers, and they have a healthy respect for Fort Union."

"They attacked stages at Point of Rocks and Wagon Mound." The fate of that little girl was ever-present in his mind, and he thought this was a good chance to find out more.

"The Fort hadn't been built then. As a matter of fact, that was one reason Colonel Sumner built it."

"Has the little girl ever been found?"

"No," answered the Lieutenant. Peter's blood ran cold at the thought of her being sold as a slave. He had heard that, if the Indians thought a boy was worth it, they would raise him as a member of their tribe. He didn't know which would be worse. It ran cold again when he was shown a hill with steep sides to the south of the road and told of a legend that, a long time ago, a number of people had died of hunger on its square top when they sought safety from an Indian attack. "That's why it's called 'Starvation Peak.'" Legend or not, the story only added to Peter's worries.

The route from Fort Union to Santa Fe passed through several small villages—Peter could neither pronounce nor understand the names. The buildings were made of rough adobe bricks; the streets were also dirt and full of broken pieces of wood. It all struck him as mean and forlorn. The feeling was added to by the mangy looking dogs that were busy scavenging for food. Brownie threatened them with deep guttural growls from the safety of his perch. They paid not the slightest attention.

By dusk it was plain that the party would not reach Santa Fe by nightfall. Lieutenant Clark decided to bivouac till morning in the ruins of the old Pecos pueblo.

"This comes of getting such a late start. If somebody had minded her own business, we could have made it in one day."

Peter felt that it would be disloyal not to defend his benefactress. "She was just trying to help me," he exclaimed with spirit. "She didn't want me to miss my Pa."

Instantly the Lieutenant was contrite. "That's all right, Pete. It won't hurt us to camp out one night."

They turned off the road to the left and rode up to the top of a low flat hill and into the ruins of a huge adobe building—it had been three stories tall. Lieutenant Clark explained that this was all that remained of what had once been the largest and most important pueblo in New Mexico.

"What's a pueblo?"

"Well, you see, some of the Indians built villages of adobe and stayed put. Instead of roaming about hunting buffalo and attacking and killing people—even scalping them—they lived by farming. This pueblo, called Pecos, was very large, with hundreds of people. For many years because they were near the plains, they traded with the Comanches and Apaches. But sometimes the Plains Indians attacked them. As if that weren't bad enough, many caught diseases brought by the Spanish and Americans and died. Not many years ago, there were so few Pecos people left that they picked up and moved, abandoned their village, and joined some of their relations in a pueblo further west on the other side of the mountains."

He showed Peter a great room that had the remains of a roof over it and explained that it had been a church built by Catholic missionaries more than a hundred years earlier.

"We'll camp in here so we won't get wet if it rains. Some people think the Indians who lived here, like Indians in Mexico, worshipped a snake-god who lived in a deep hole. I don't know about that, but there's a lot of un-Godly snakes here now; so look out for rattlers. However, they hole in after dark when it gets cold, and we'll be gone by the time they come out to warm themselves."

Peter did not sleep much that night, but it was not fear of rattlesnakes that kept him awake. He was too excited. The nearer he got to Santa Fe, the more panicky he grew. All night long he twisted and tossed under his blankets. He was so eager to see his father and at the same time so fearful that he would miss him that he could not settle down. On the other hand, Brownie had no such worries and enjoyed the deep sleep of a worn-out dog.

When morning came at last, Peter thought they would never get started. He became very impatient and, although he did not show it to anyone but poor unoffending Brownie, very irritable, which was not at all like him. Finally, all the chores had been completed, and everyone mounted up. They were off.

"Well, Pete, only about twenty-five miles more. We'll be there before you know it." But Peter was so tense that he silently disagreed. It seemed to him that the cavalry horses were just creeping along. He was not a good judge of distances, and twenty-five miles meant little to him. As they rounded every bend in the road and emerged from every canyon, he peered ahead expectantly, hoping that the fabled City of the Holy Faith would lie spread out before his eager eyes in all the glory with which his imagination had endowed it. He looked for a city of silver and gold with broad tree-lined avenues and imposing marble palaces. No one had ever thought to tell him that Santa Fe simply was not like that— in fact, mostly made of mud.

Then, all of a sudden, there it was. The sight came as quite a shock. There was no silver or gold or marble. It was just a larger edition of the miserable little towns they had been hurrying through since leaving

Fort Union, row after row of crumbling adobe houses dominated by the twin towers of a big church, which he hardly noticed. And it was for a place like this that Pa had left St. Louis! However, if he were still here, nothing else would matter. He did see that the city was in a wide valley with mountains on each side, those on the right almost touching the road, the others far away to the west.

The company rode rapidly down a long slope into one of the narrow streets, but Peter thought even that was not fast enough. When they entered the town, the Lieutenant tried to interest him in the strings of bright red peppers that hung by every door and in the aroma coming from scores of piñon pine fires. But he was too wrapped up in his own thoughts to care about such trivial things. He wanted to rush on ahead, but now that the long-awaited moment was at hand, he longed to hold back.

After a few minutes, they emerged from the narrow ugly street into a large open square, and he blinked in the dazzling sunlight. The rest of the troop clattered on while the Lieutenant reined in his horse before a long railing to which other horses were already tied, and Peter pulled Pluto in beside him. Raising his eyes, he saw a large sign which read, "Spiegelberg Bros., Mchdse." Here at last was the spot, the goal he had dreamed about for weeks. They dismounted and tied their ponies to the railing.

"Come on," said the Lieutenant and disappeared through the narrow door beneath the sign. Peter felt a little faint, but he followed, with Brownie right behind him.

When they were inside, half-blinded because their eyes had not adjusted to the darkness, he could see nothing but a black-bearded man standing behind a counter. He strained his eyes for a familiar face and waited for an astonished cry of "Peter!" But nothing happened.

Lieutenant Clark approached the counter. "Morning, Sol," he said.

"Morning, Fred," replied the bearded man.

"Abel here?"

"Abel Blair? No, he left town yesterday morning. Can I do anything for you?"

The Lieutenant laid a hand on his charge's shoulder. "Where'd he go—California?"

Santa Fe—At Last

"No. Up to Taos on some business of mine. From there he's going back to St. Louis to get a youngster of his."

It had taken a moment for the dreadful news to sink into Peter's consciousness, but now it did with an awful force. All the emotions he had been able to bottle up inside during the past weeks burst forth. He turned to the wall, buried his face in his arm, and gave way to hysterical sobbing.

Mr. Spiegelberg stared at him.

"This is that youngster. He's come all the way out over the Trail to find his father. And now this! It's pretty rough."

The proprietor, full of sympathy, came out from behind the counter and crossed to the weeping boy.

"Yes, that's certainly too bad," he said. "It's a cruel shame. But maybe we can reach him before he starts East. Taos isn't very far, and it'll take him two or three days to finish my business. Yes, we must try to get word to him."

"Let's take Mrs. Bowen's advice," said the Lieutenant, "and go see the Governor. If anybody can help us, he can. Let's go. Goodbye, Sol, and keep your ears open."

Together they crossed the hot dusty plaza to a long low building with a porch—Peter would learn to call it a portal. After going in through the wide front door, they were met by a tall black man who seemed to be keeping an eye on a number of Indians and Mexicans who were sitting stolidly on a bench against the wall.

"Morning, Frank," the Lieutenant greeted him.

"Mornin', Lieutenant." the man replied respectfully.

"Governor in?"

"In there." He pointed toward a room on the left.

"Is he busy? Can he see us?"

Frank shook his head disapprovingly. "He's always busy. But I reckon he'll take time to see you." He looked searchingly at Peter. "Walk right in."

They entered a spacious, scantily furnished room. A large elderly gentleman was seated behind a table listening intently while a much smaller man, who stood at his elbow, interpreted what a worried looking Mexican with a large sombrero in his hands was saying with great seriousness. Fortunately the conversation was soon over and, after a deep bow, the Mexican departed.

"Well, Lieutenant, what can I do for you?" the Governor inquired cordially, if a bit wearily.

"Nothing special for me, sir. Here is your petitioner." The Lieutenant put his arm over Peter's shoulder. "He is a fellow citizen of yours, Peter Blair of St. Louis, and he's in great trouble. Pete, suppose you tell the Governor what your trouble is."

After one look at the boy's stricken face, Governor Lane held out his arms and drew him between his knees. Responding to this warmth and sympathy, the boy buried his face in the large vest and sobbed. The Governor held him close, and if Peter had been in any condition to notice, he would have seen that the old gentleman's eyes were moist.

"Come on, Peter," he said, "tell me what's wrong. I have a very soft place in my heart for little boys, and I'll do everything I can to help you."

By this time Frank had come in from the hall and joined the Lieutenant and the interpreter in listening attentively as Peter stammered out his story. When he had finally finished, the Governor seated him on his knee.

"Well, Peter, the end of the world has not come yet, though," he added hastily, "it does seem like it to you. We all have our disappointments, and I'm sure you'll live to have others. But they always seem hopeless when they come, especially if we're very young. The thing to do right away is to find someone who is going to Taos and can get word to your Pa."

"Please, sir, I want to go too. Please!!"

"Of course you do. But we'll have to see about that. I can't let you go without an adequate guard. Right now I have a posse out searching for a little Mexican boy the Navajos carried off two weeks ago. I'm not going to run any risks with you."

"But that was in the back country," put in the smaller man. "The highway is perfectly safe. Look at all the traffic going and coming every day. No Navajo has shown his face on it for months—nor Apache either."

"Nevertheless, I don't propose to take any chances. Peter, you'll just have to trust in me. If anything happened to you, I'd never know a moment's peace again in my life. And how could I face your pa? Excuse me, this is Mr. Otero, my secretary. And that is Frank Smith, who came with me from St. Louis and is always ordering me around." Then he turned to Lieutenant Clark. "When are you to report back to Fort Union?"

"Orders are for tomorrow."

"Well, orders are orders, and I can't change them, no matter how much I want to, even if I am supposed to be in charge."

At this moment Peter's attention was attracted by a noise in the vestibule. All the waiting Mexicans and Indians were getting to their feet and bowing respectfully to a dignified man in what he recognized as clerical dress. He slid from the Governor's knee as the latter rose to welcome his caller.

"Honored to see you, Your Reverence," he said, extending his hand across the table. "Frank, fetch a seat for Bishop Lamy."

Frank obeyed and the Bishop, first smoothing out the folds of his cassock, settled himself comfortably.

"You know Mike Otero of course, and this is Lieutenant . . . Excuse an old man's bad memory."

"Clark," said the Lieutenant.

"And this is Peter Blair, a fellow-citizen of mine all the way from St. Louis."

The Bishop leaned across the table and shook hands with great gravity. In so doing he spied the little medal Father Donahue had hung around Peter's neck on the levee. He reached over and fingered it approvingly.

"And where did you get this?" he asked.

"Father Donahue gave it to me. He's sort of a priest I know in St. Louis."

"Is he your pastor?"

Peter did not know the answer to this question, so Mr. Otero came to his rescue.

"His Reverence means, do you go to his church?"

"Oh no, sir. He just helped me when I was having a fight about Brownie." He pointed to the little dog, who was sitting unnoticed by the wall. "Mrs. Morris, the lady I lived with, goes to the Methodist church, and she takes me with her. I don't know what I am. You'll have to ask Pa."

162

Even the Bishop smiled. "I'll have to do just that. As the good Governor knows, there are many roads to Heaven. Take good care of the medal, and it will take good care of you."

The Governor then explained Peter's—and his—dilemma.

"I think I can help. You came at just the right time. I know of a party starting for Taos in the morning, and you can go with them."

"Who are they?" asked the Governor.

"Some very reliable men from my parish. Mr. Otero, you know Juan Batista, a very devout young man. He's the leader."

Otero nodded.

"How many will be in the party? Will they be armed?" The Governor was not wholly satisfied yet. "Your Reverence must excuse me for asking so many questions, but I am responsible for the boy's safety."

"There will be twelve or fifteen, and they will be well armed. The only trouble is that none of them speak English. That will, I admit, be a little awkward for Peter unless he speaks Spanish, but it won't be serious."

Peter shook his head. "No, sir."

He turned to the Governor. "They mean to make it in two days. They'll sleep at Embudo. And from there it's not far to Taos—less than twenty-five miles."

Governor Lane was obviously not yet easy in his mind. "Over the worst road in the world. I know it."

"There's a short cut up a trail," volunteered the Lieutenant.

"I know that, too. It's even worse. Then there's another thing. Suppose Mr. Blair isn't in Taos. Who'll look after Peter?"

Peter had thought of that, but dared not mention it. At this point he was ready to take any risk so long as he was safe from capture by Indians.

"I have many friends who will be happy to," said the Bishop. Still the Governor hesitated.

Seeing this, Peter cried out in impassioned tones, "Please let me go! Please!"

Again Mr. Otero came to the rescue. "He'll be perfectly safe, I'm sure."

"Of course he will," interrupted the prelate. "These are all good people. Now I must be off. I just dropped in to pay my respects. Be sure to be at the Exchange Hotel at five-thirty tomorrow morning, and the next day you'll be in your dear father's arms."

They all rose to their feet, and he departed.

The Governor busied himself absent-mindedly with some papers on his table. The others waited respectfully for his decision.

"I still don't like it. The Bishop is a very good man—we all know that—but good men are sometimes easily fooled—and he hasn't been here very long."

"Please, sir," cried Peter, "I'm not afraid!"

"I know you're not. But I am. If this Batista is such a reliable man, he can be entrusted to take a message to Mr. Blair."

Peter, the tears coursing down his cheeks, turned to his best friend, Brownie, for comfort.

The Governor was deeply moved. "I don't care what you all say. I am not going to take a chance of this boy's being carried off into captivity, never to be heard of again! It's happened too often. I know what it is to lose an only son, and I'm not going to inflict such devastation on this boy's father! Mike," he added after he had got hold of himself, "you talk to your friend Batista, and report back to me."

The young man departed, and so too did Lieutenant Clark. Then the harassed Governor turned to his servant.

"Take this young man and give him a good dinner. I don't want any."

But Frank did not move.

164 "Yes, you do. Anyway, I've got it all ready for you an' you're goin' to eat it. The two of you sit right down at that table. I don' want to hear any more about not bein' hungry."

After firing that broadside, he left the room with great dignity.

"Well, Peter, you see who's the real governor of New Mexico. We must do as we are told. It seems to me that everybody is part of a conspiracy to make me do what I don't want to."

The boy took a seat at the table.

"You're one of them, Peter, and it's terribly hard to say no. Now here's Frank with our dinner. So let's obey orders. But first we must give thanks to the Doer of All Good who has brought you safely through so many hardships and dangers—and who has provided us with the dinner which Frank has cooked so well."

Chapter Thirteen

"It was Mistuh Chaves who provided the venison."

"We'll not argue that point, but eat it gratefully, no matter who provided it. Master Peter here needs a good meal under his belt."

"So do you."

This sally was ignored and a suitable blessing was pronounced by Governor Lane. "And so, if I am not mistaken, does . . . what's your pet's name?"

"Brownie, sir."

"Brownie needs a dinner too, though I can't see that he is wearing a belt. But never mind that. Just give him the fat of the land. I'm sure he deserves it."

Reluctant as he was to leave his master, the temptation of the bone Frank held out to him was too great, and Brownie allowed himself to be led from the room.

Both the Governor and Frank had been right, and the two plates were soon empty. As they ate, the boy and the man talked about St. Louis. Peter was surprised at how much the Governor enjoyed the description of the city by a young boy.

After dinner, the Governor turned his guest over to Frank.

"Show this young gentleman the town. Bring him back for supper, and then fix him a pallet in my room. I'm sorry we don't have enough beds to go 'round in this misnamed Palace, but we don't, and so we have to make do with what we have. I'll be busy here. Those patient people are still waiting to see me, everyone with a favor to ask. By the way, don't let Brownie get into trouble. There are plenty of ornery curs in this town." He took Peter's two hands in his and squeezed and patted them. Then he dismissed Frank and Peter.

Frank was a good guide. Nevertheless, the sightseeing tour was not a great success. The supposed tourist had his mind on other things, and he was not interested in the curiosities of Santa Fe, nor its contrasts with St. Louis. When they got back to the Palace, they found not only Mr. Otero but also Lieutenant Clark and Mr. Spiegelberg in the Governor's office.

"You see, Peter," said Mr. Otero, "what an important person you are."

He was reporting that he had just seen Señor Batista and that he had declared himself more than happy to act as escort and bodyguard. He, too, was in a great hurry to reach Taos, and would press on as fast as possible. There would not be the slightest danger.

The Lieutenant had met some fellow officers who had just come down. They reported that the Indians had all been chased into the mountains west of the river. They were confident that there were none remaining east of it.

So far as Peter was concerned, the most interesting contribution was Mr. Spiegelberg's. One of his employees had just ridden down from Taos all alone and had not had the slightest trouble. But what was really important was that he had seen "Pa," who reported that he could hardly wait to start East and get his son. He planned to start Friday. This was Tuesday; so there was no time to lose.

It was evident to all that the Governor was far from happy. After a moment's silence, he said, "Well, I know when I'm licked. Peter, you win. You have my permission to go."

"Oh, thank you, sir! I'll be all right." He ran over to his benefactor and gazed up into his eyes. "I really will, sir. I promise."

The Governor grasped his shoulders and looked down into the boy's eyes. He tried to speak, but could not, and without a word walked quickly from the room. Peter started to follow him, but was stopped by Frank, who said: "Leave him be. He'll be all right in a minute, he's thinking of his son who died a few years ago. Wasn't much older than you."

The Lieutenant said, "I'll have your pony at the Exchange in plenty of time." Then he followed Mr. Spiegelberg out of the building.

Frank was right. The Governor returned shortly in full control of himself, but unsmiling.

"Mike, write a letter to Señora Valdez. Give her my compliments and tell her that Peter will be spending tomorrow night in Embudo. Ask her to take him in and look after him."

"Yes, sir," replied the Secretary and he took his leave.

The two St. Louisans had their supper together, but unlike their dinner, it was a silent repast, both being too preoccupied for casual conversation.

Not long after they had finished, Peter retired to his pallet on the floor of the Governor's bedroom. He tried to go to sleep, but it was a long time before he succeeded. In the first place, he had become used to sleeping in the open air and found the room very hot and stuffy. Then too, when the Governor finally left his work and lay down on his cot, he tossed for some time. When he did finally settle down, his loud snores rivaled those of Uncle Seth. Frank rigged up an improvised bed across the open doorway, and quickly joined his master in concert. Peter wondered how old he would be when he started to make noises like that.

When he was finally wakened by Frank, it was still dark, and it took him a couple of minutes to remember where he was. After another good breakfast, he was ready to go. First, he wanted to say goodbye to his friend, the Governor, but he was still asleep, and Frank would not let him be disturbed. So, feeling a trifle ungrateful, he took off under Frank's guidance across the Plaza to the Exchange, which Frank informed him was "a kinda hotel."

They found half a dozen mules standing patiently in front of it by the hitching-rail while several men weighed them down with packs filled with merchandise. One man stood out from the rest—slim, handsome, young, richly dressed in Mexican finery, and wearing a very showy black and gold sombrero. He kept pacing back and forth and consulting a large gold watch. There could be no doubt that he was angry.

Presently he was joined by Mr. Otero, who tried without conspicuous success to calm him down, for he continued to wave his arms wildly. This was not the best moment for introductions, but maybe "Mike" hoped to distract him. In any event, he led Peter up and presented him to "Señor Batista." Brownie followed and sat by his master's right heel. Señor Batista managed an indifferent greeting. When, however, his eyes lit on the unoffending little animal, his indifference disappeared in a hurry. He pointed angrily at him and exploded, "No! No! No!"

The upshot was that, while he had no objection to taking a boy in tow, he would not take a dog. That was final.

"Mike" broke the news to Peter with some embarrassment, for Mr. Batista was not exactly living up to his advance notices. He explained that the Señor was upset because several members of his party had not yet shown up and were delaying everything. He was very anxious to reach Taos at the earliest possible moment, and anger had overcome his good nature.

This was a body blow to Peter. He had never been separated from Brownie for more than a few hours since they had joined forces three years before. Had the circumstances been different, he would have backed out, but such a refusal was unthinkable. Frank, who, he suspected, was not well-impressed by Mr. Batista, assured him that he would be back in a few days and that he and Governor Lane would take good care of the little dog, with whom he was now on the best of terms. He inquired why the party was not using burros as pack animals and was told they were too slow.

In about fifteen minutes the missing men appeared with their mules and horses, only to be greeted with such a tongue-lashing that for a few minutes it looked as if they were going to refuse to go. However, the good-natured Mr. Otero was able to restore order and peace.

Just then Lieutenant Clark appeared with a soldier leading Pluto. Peter, anxious not to bring down any wrath on his head, mounted in a hurry. It was more than he could do to tell Brownie goodbye, and as the party started off, he looked straight ahead and tried to ignore the big lump in his throat. But he managed to wave to Mr. Spiegelberg, who was standing by his door to see them off.

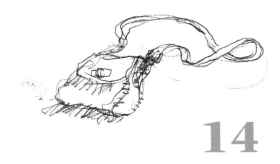

14

The Governor Was Right

They soon left Santa Fe behind as the horses trotted up the dusty road leading north. They saw so many people that Peter decided the Governor must have been wrong about any dangers lurking nearby. Mr. Batista, his anger having subsided, kept up a steady conversation, quite oblivious to the fact that his listener could understand almost nothing he said. He swept his sombrero off with a flourish when they passed a young lady in a cart. Then when they met a priest, he made what Peter recognized as the sign of the cross. Next he pointed toward a collection of low adobe houses to the left of the road—"Tesuque Pueblo—ver' old." Later he gestured toward the bluish mountains to the west and said, "Rio Grande." Peter knew enough to understand that he was referring, not to the mountains, but to the river which flowed at their base. He was fascinated by the odd shapes of the rock formations close to the road, one of which resembled the pictures he had seen of camels.

He found the day's ride, though interesting, quite tiring and was very glad when, about dusk, they halted at a small settlement only slightly less forlorn than others they had passed. A white-haired lady dressed entirely in black was standing in front of the largest house, which had been painted pink, and was lighting the candle in a lantern which hung by the front door.

Springing from his horse, Mr. Batista greeted her gaily. She welcomed him with a pleasant smile and a few words spoken in a low voice. Peter also dismounted at a sign from him and was led to her with the letter from Mr. Otero. He was sure this was Señora Valdez. She fished a pair of steel-rimmed glasses from her pocket and read the note intently. When she had finished, she folded it carefully, and then embraced Peter. Of course, he could not understand any of the Spanish words, but gathered that both he and Mr. Batista were invited to spend the night in her house. Beckoning him to follow, Mr. Batista led the way to a small stable, in which he locked the two horses, and left them contentedly munching oats. Peter caught a glimpse of the other Mexicans, who had gathered near another house with their horses and mules.

The Señora served a supper of fried corn meal cakes, which Mr. Batista told Peter were tortillas, beans (frijoles), and delicious sweet peaches. The tortillas and the frijoles were both doused with red-hot chili which scorched Peter's mouth, but which he quickly learned to like. She also offered him coffee, but he politely declined.

Soon after supper had been finished, Mr. Batista's good humor was speedily put to an end to by loud noises that emanated from outside. They were obviously the sounds of a raucous party. He leaped to his feet with a curse that shocked his hostess and then rushed outside. Señora Valdez shook her white head disapprovingly as she spread out two mattresses on the floor. The quiet of the night was broken by angry shouts and drunken singing. When Mr. Batista came back, he was in such a foul temper that Peter hastily lay down on his improvised bed to get out of his way, and the lady, finding herself powerless to stop the fury, retired from the room. For some time the irate young man paced the floor, occasionally kicking at the furniture. Eventually he exhausted himself and followed the good example set by his charge.

If Mr. Batista's anger the night before had been awe-inspiring, it was nothing compared to the display he put on in the morning. After returning to the kitchen from a tour of inspection, he yelled so loudly that he set all the dogs within earshot to barking. All Embudo was in an uproar. His hostess raised her eyes to heaven and repeatedly made the sign of the cross. His gold watch was hauled out half a dozen times and held under her nose. Each time she looked at Peter and shook her head hopelessly. Yet somehow she managed to serve them breakfast, more tortillas, peaches, and coffee, which this time Peter did not spurn.

Chapter Fourteen

When everything in sight had been consumed, a quarrel broke out between the two adults, and Peter realized uncomfortably that it was centered on him.

Señora Valdez put her arms protectively about him and kept repeating, "No! No!" There was more, much more that he could not understand. It ended only when the angry man almost tore him from her arms. She kissed the little medal hanging about his neck and made the sign of the cross over and over again. Once outdoors, Peter quickly discovered what had sparked his companion's explosion. The men who rode the horses and mules were sleeping off their orgy instead of being ready to start. Mr. Batista's curses and his well-aimed kicks elicited only grunts. Señora Valdez came from the house, unlocked the stable, and indicated a tank of water, to which Peter led Pluto. After more futile protests, she stood by, wringing her hands, and murmuring prayers. Again she kissed the little medal hanging about Peter's neck and both his cheeks. Then he and Mr. Batista were off.

The trail was rough, and Pluto picked his way so carefully that Mr. Batista repeatedly turned in his saddle and motioned for him to speed up. Once when they met a string of heavy-laden and stumbling burros driven by two boys, they had to step off the narrow trail to let them pass. The boys didn't seem to hear the curses that rained down on them.

Before they had gone very far, Mr. Batista turned and started up an even more forbidding trail that led up the steep eastern side of the canyon—no doubt this was the one the Governor had said was so bad. It was, in fact, so steep and rocky that even Mr. Batista was unable to compel his horse to climb as quickly as he wanted him to. But by dint of constant spurring and beating with his whip, the young man forced his horse on. Pluto simply could not keep up. Peter was left behind to fend for himself. He did his utmost to speed Pluto up, but the distance separating him from Mr. Batista steadily grew greater. He did not like this at all, but there was nothing he could do about it. He could not help thinking how upset the Governor would be.

They rode on like this and finally came into a grove of spruce trees that had somehow managed to find enough soil to stay alive among the many huge boulders which had rolled down the canyon side. At last, after they had gone on in this way for a couple of hours, the trail leveled off somewhat. Peter had not been able to catch up, but then heard the ringing of church bells. They were a long way off, but at least there was a settlement not too far away. Maybe it was Taos at last. He thought he was safe.

But suddenly, he felt someone jump behind him on Pluto's back!

He screamed in terror, but a rough hand was clamped over his mouth. Mr. Batista whirled in his saddle, took one look, and instantly dug his spurs into his horse's sides—not to come to Peter's rescue, but to escape to Taos. He disappeared around a bend.

Although he could not see his captor, Peter had no doubt he was an Indian. He would not have known he was an Apache even if he had seen him. He did not have to wait to have his fear confirmed. Pluto was wheeled about abruptly and ridden up to the shelter of a great boulder. Here the Indian stopped and slipped to the ground, dragging the terrified boy after him. He was tall and wore only a pair of weather-beaten trousers covered with dust. His glistening black hair was drawn to the back of his head and tied in a knot above his neck. Both a large pistol and a murderous looking knife were attached to his belt. He pulled the knife from its sheath and held it against Peter's throat. There could be no doubt what he meant, though Peter could not understand his grunts.

He was very strong—and very rough. He jerked Peter's arms and tied his wrists behind him. Then he threw Peter up on Pluto's rump and sprang into the saddle. He wound another rope around Peter's waist and then about his own. It was pulled so tight that it hurt, but Peter was too wise to cry out. He remembered all the warnings he had heard about showing any sign of weakness if captured by Indians.

Once in the saddle, the Apache rode Pluto off the trail and back along the side of the canyon, but there were so many loose rocks and so many trees growing close together that he could not make a fast escape. The viciousness with which Pluto was spurred made his master's blood boil. He was wild with both fury and terror, but managed to control himself and keep quiet. He was certain that his captor wanted to escape, but could not decide what was the safest way to go. Every few minutes he stopped to listen and look about in all directions. All Peter could hear was the yelping of a distant coyote.

172

The Apache continued south and moved cautiously along the slope, jerking Pluto furiously every time one of his feet dislodged a loose stone that rolled noisily down the hill.

The memory of the Ugly Boy and the kidnapped girl raced through Peter's mind. It would not have helped to have known that it was the Apaches who were thought to have committed the murders at both Wagon Mound and Point of Rocks—nor that a band of them under their chief, Chacon, was camped 50 miles to the west. They had come to receive food under a treaty with the U.S. Government, but the government had dishonored the agreement and not delivered the food. The Indians wanted revenge—and with good reason.

The most horrible of fates had overtaken Peter. How right the Governor and Señora Valdez had been! He could imagine how horrified they would be when they heard the news. And poor little Brownie waiting in the Palace for the master he might never see again! But most of all he thought of Pa, and of what the Governor had said of the loss of an only son. He was not consoled by the thought that the Governor would send out all the available troops to find him.

While this went through his mind, they entered a grove of trees that was clinging to the soil at the base of a sheer rock wall. The Apache pulled Pluto up short. He thought that his captor wanted to get across the Rio Grande to the safety of the other side. It looked as if the Indian planned to go down the side of the canyon and make a dash across the river. He turned the pony's head sharply to the right, and started cautiously down the hill. Peter gave up all hope.

Then Pluto neighed.

The Indian pulled him back so short that his haunches almost touched the ground. Unused to such treatment he reared up and neighed again and again. It was like a cry for help.

A chorus of answers came from the trail. The men who had so infuriated Mr. Batista by oversleeping appeared from around the bend. The Mexicans looked through the trees and saw Pluto. Peter hoped they had also seen him. They all shouted in excitement as the Indian jerked Pluto about.

As fast as he could maneuver Pluto, the Apache sought shelter in the

173

The Governor Was Right

trees while he decided which way to escape. He was confronted by a cliff on the left that no horse could climb and the armed Mexicans coming up the trail. He leaped from the horse and threw the rope-bound boy to the ground. Now other voices came from above—he was cornered. Three men appeared at the top of the cliff. He drew his pistol from his belt and fired at them. They disappeared. He then dragged his helpless captive to the foot of the rock and stood with his back to it, holding Peter with one arm in front of him as a shield. He held the pistol with his free hand.

He had not, however, chosen a good place for self-defense. A shower of loose rocks, dirt, and sand poured down on them as the men scrambled to get down. Peter was protected by his broad-brimmed hat, but his captor had nothing on his head and was blinded. When he put his hand to his eyes, Peter broke loose and stumbled a few feet away, but with his arms still bound could not keep his balance on the slope and fell down.

The Indian could see again and reached for the pistol he had dropped. As he straightened up, the sharp crack of a rifle rang out. Peter saw the Apache spin about and fall on his face.

Peter struggled to his feet. Several men raced toward him—he recognized one.

"Pa! Pa!"

His father stopped short. He couldn't believe what he thought he saw. He came on slowly at first. Finally—

"Peter! Peter!"

He seized the boy in his arms.

"Peter, what are you doing here?"

"I came to find you. Uncle Seth brought me. But he's sick at Fort Union."

His father undid the rope. There were tears in his eyes and his hands trembled.

"I galloped from Taos to help rescue a boy I heard had been carried off by the Apaches, and find it's my own son! I thought he was in St. Louis!"

No one spoke. Then, kicking the dead Indian, one of them said, "What he was really after was the horse. The youngster was lucky." He looked

Peter saw the Apache spin about
        and fall on his face.

at Peter, "You must have a good luck charm."

"I do," Peter answered and pulled the little medal from underneath his shirt.

His father took it in his fingers. "Where did you get this?"

"Father Donahue, a kind of priest, gave it to me just as I was gettin' on the boat. He said it would bring me good luck. He was right. It did. Now I want to get Brownie."

"Brownie! Where's he?"

"In Santa Fe. The Governor's taking care of him."

15

Peter and Brownie Reunited

When Peter had awakened that morning on Señora Valdez's floor, all he could think of was Pa—and the chance he might have already left for St. Louis. He had not thought at all about the Ugly Boy and kidnapped girl—yet, in a few hours, he would be thinking only of them.

His father got up in Taos at about the same time; his thoughts were only of getting to St. Louis to get Peter. He could not have imagined that Peter was a few miles away and soon to be in great danger. He had completed the business for Mr. Spiegelberg and planned to start the long trip to St. Louis the next day. He was going to go over the mountains, down the valley to Mora, and on to Ft. Union to wait for a wagon train headed east.

Now, however, that the adventures of the morning were over—the Apache had been buried with his scalp still on—both Peter and his father were let down and exhausted. His father decided to return to Señora Valdez's hacienda for the night. He felt quite safe making the short trip, because any other raiding Indians in the area would have been scared off. He had heard that a small troop of soldiers was leaving Taos for Santa Fe before daybreak the following day; so he and Peter could join them as they went by Embudo.

Both Peter and Pluto were sore because of the rough treatment they had received at the hands of the Apache, but neither had serious injuries. Peter's vocal cords were not in any way damaged, though they became weary as he related every detail of his trip from St. Louis to Santa Fe.

He started with the encounter with Aleck on the levee, described the fight over Brownie, Uncle Seth's arrival at Mrs. Morris's, and on and on. He only paused when they returned down the steepest part of the trail and could not ride abreast.

They arrived at Señora Valdez's shortly after the sun went down—and at the Pecos Pueblo in Peter's narrative. Señora Valdez rushed out, gathered Peter in her arms, and hugged him until he could hardly breathe. She had heard of the attempted kidnapping, but fortunately had heard of the rescue at the same time. She was spared the agony of thinking she might have saved Peter from an awful fate.

Soon after their arrival, she served them the same dinner as the night before—she had gotten no new supplies. But Peter was too tired and excited to notice, though he did think he liked chili better every time he had it.

They all went to sleep quickly—there were no noisy and drinking revelers. Pluto and "Pa's" grey mare, Sam, had been put in the barn and were happily eating oats. As Peter went to sleep, he thought he would try to remember to ask why a mare was named "Sam."

Peter was still tired when he woke up in the morning as the sun came over the mountains. For weeks he had thought only of finding his father. Being with him was even better than he had imagined, but he now wondered what it would be like living in Santa Fe. Nobody had told him about all those brown buildings. He wondered where they would live, how Brownie would deal with the mean looking dogs he had seen in the streets. He also wondered about Pluto—he wanted to keep him and not send him on another trip on the Trail where he might be stolen by Comanches.

Pa was also uncertain. He had planned to bring his son back to Santa Fe the following spring, and Mr. Spiegelberg had promised there would be a job for him. The business was growing rapidly; so he hoped he would be needed right away. He also worried about finding a bigger place to live, but he didn't tell Peter about any of this.

The six mounted soldiers were returning to Santa Fe after accompanying a coach to Taos three days earlier. Another group would ride north, spend four days in Taos, and bring the coach back in two weeks. Taos was becoming more civilized, but both the Governor and Col. Sumner thought that, because of the violence six years earlier, it was a good idea to have soldiers in Taos on a regular basis. That was one of the few things they agreed on.

The troop set off from Embudo shortly after nine and made good time as they headed for Santa Fe. Peter had finished the description of his trip to Santa Fe at dinner the previous night, including the meeting and meals with Governor Lane. "He hugged just like you, Pa."

Pa couldn't keep his eyes off Peter. "He is a fine man, was mayor of St. Louis for many years."

Fortunately, the Governor, just as Señora Valdez, had heard of Peter's capture and rescue at the same time. He didn't know what to think—his instincts in not wanting Peter to go had been correct, but if he had not gone, he would have missed his father in Taos. He was sure Bishop Lamy would think it divine providence, but the Governor thought the Bishop still had much to learn about life in New Mexico.

The Governor had also heard that Peter and his father were on their way to Santa Fe and would arrive late that afternoon. He was sure they would come straight to the Palace—to see Brownie!

They did. The reunion was something to see—the blur of a brown dog running in circles was interrupted only by leaps into Peter's arms. Finally after five minutes, Brownie sniffed "Pa's" legs and started the whole process over. The Governor, Frank, and Mr. Otero watched all this alternately smiling and laughing—there wasn't a dry eye in the room. They even clapped and said over and over, "It's a wonder."

179

The Governor turned to Peter and his father. "I knew you would be hungry and need a place to sleep tonight; so I had Frank make enough room for two cots and prepare a St. Louis feast—or as close as we can come at this distance. I've also asked Sol Spiegelberg to come, though even Frank couldn't arrange for German food."

Frank was able to get two chickens and a mutton leg. He boiled the chicken, roasted the mutton, and served them with a huge dish of mashed squash, corn cut off the cob and mixed with chili—the one New Mexico dish—piles of hot biscuits, and sweet apple pie. Peter had three glasses of milk, while the others had dark red wine.

Peter and Brownie Reunited

A small troop of soldiers had arrived from Ft. Union earlier in the afternoon with the mail stage. They reported that Uncle Seth and Aleck had started the same morning for Santa Fe. Kitty Bowen had worked her magic on her new "cousin," and Uncle Seth was raring to get going to see Peter—and hoped he wouldn't have to look after him further. He didn't think Peter should return on the Trail with him—and he knew he couldn't settle down in Santa Fe.

The room in the Palace of the Governors was barely big enough to hold the table with the five men around it and to allow Frank, who was helped by the Governor's Indian interpreter from Tesuque, José Maria, to serve the meal. The conversation during dinner amounted to little more than, "Pass the squash." "I'll have one more piece of mutton." "I can eat one more biscuit." "Three pieces of pie isn't too much." "Want another piece of meat, Brownie?" Peter had not said all those things, but many of them.

Frank was generous with the wine, and the men started talking about Santa Fe. Sol Spiegelberg had arrived six years earlier and started trading. "Lots has changed since then. One brother came last year and another's coming next. More people all the time. Abel, we'll need your help, and Peter can help clean up. May be a little tame after the Trail, but might not be so bad."

Governor Lane had heard all Peter's talk about ferocious Indians and scalping and knew that many were that way. "Peter, that Apache scared me as much as you when I heard about him. You always have to be careful, and I'm sure you will. Not everybody is so lucky. But the Pueblo Indians are different, live in civilized communities, each governed by its own laws, subject to the Governor of the Territory." He laughed and pointed at himself. "That's me. Indians are like Americans—some good, some not so good. But I'm glad you didn't wind up as one of them."

He went on, "It sounds as though your father's got a good job. The Bishop is starting schools; so you'll have something to do to keep you and Brownie from running around getting into fights."

Peter and his father just kept turning and looking at each other. It hadn't all sunk in yet, but they had found each other—and were not going to be separated again.

Chapter Fifteen

Brownie was sound asleep—snoring. Peter thought he must have learned that from Uncle Seth. He knew they both would be waiting in the Plaza to greet Uncle Seth and Aleck and tell them about the trip to Taos, the Apache, and that he and Pa were going to live in Santa Fe.

He could imagine Uncle Seth. "You're a good'un. So's yer dog. 'Tween yer Pa and me, we'll keep you 'way from Injuns and keep Brownie out of the pot. Anyways, you'll be aw'right—you're a trail man." Peter could imagine Uncle Seth's eyes twinkling—and he smiled.

Peter and Brownie Reunited

Afterword

The story in this book was conceived over sixty years ago, but it was not finished until the mid-1960s, when it appeared as *Peter and Brownie Follow the Trace, a Story of the Santa Fe Trail*. The original boy became Peter in honor of my father's first grandchild. Peter's mentor, Seth, was named after my wife's father. Brownie remained unchanged. He had been named after a small brown dog and beloved pet that Bruce, my older brother and Peter's father, and I had during the 1930s in St. Louis.

The account of a twelve-year-old boy's trip from St. Louis to Santa Fe in the summer of 1853 in search of his father includes an accurate description of many landmarks along the Santa Fe Trail. While the principal characters making the trip are fictional, many of the others are not, including the New Mexico Territorial Governor, Wm. Carr Lane, his secretary Miguel A. Otero, and his servant, Frank Smith. The day-to-day activities provide an accurate portrayal of life at that time and of the hardships encountered on a trip from St. Louis to Santa Fe—and then on toward Taos. Many of the landmarks can still be found. Even now, one can well imagine Peter at Pawnee Rock, later being scrubbed under the supervision of Kitty Bowen—another real character—while Uncle Seth was incapacitated at Ft. Union, and finally eating dinner with the governor in the Palace of the Governors in Santa Fe. Throughout the story the dialogue accurately represents how people used—and abused—language, including some of the derogatory terms common to the mid-nineteenth century.

My father, William Glasgow Bruce Carson, lived in St. Louis all his life, except for several years in France during World War I and in Ames at the start of his teaching career at Iowa State University. He joined the English Department at Washington University in St. Louis in 1919 and remained there until his retirement in 1956. He and my mother continued to live in their house on Maryland Avenue across from the campus until his death in 1976 and hers in 1983. They had been married fifty-three years. Their lives in many ways revolved around the university, and he always had a deep love of St. Louis. His family had lived there for generations.

He had carefully reviewed the journal Dr. Lane kept during the trip to Santa Fe and later published those covering the ten months from February 28, 1853, to December 25, 1853, in the *New Mexico Historical Review*, (October 1964). As a twelve-year-old in 1903, he and his mother had accompanied Mrs. Western Bascom, a daughter of Stephen Watts Kearney, to Santa Fe to present a portrait of the General to the Historical Society. It still hangs in the Palace of the Governors. The world had changed drastically in the fifty years that elapsed between the trip of the fictional twelve-year-old and the real one—the railroad had replaced wagons on the Santa Fe Trail and Indians were not a threat.

During the 1930s, our immediate family traveled to Santa Fe during four summers, one year carefully following the Trail in a 1934 Pontiac. Brownie did not come. Bruce and I spent summers at the boys' camp at the Los Alamos Ranch School prior to World War II. During those years, my father did further research in New Mexico, including talking at various times to former Governor Miguel Antonio Otero, the son of Wm. Carr Lane's secretary.

I don't know exactly when he first had the idea for the story nor when he actually started writing, but I do know that he completed it in 1965 at the urging of the real Peter. At that time, Peter, who is now a San Francisco attorney, was growing up with his parents in a St. Louis suburb. He did not have to make a long trek to see his father.

My own interest in the story was re-kindled in 1992 when my wife, Georgia, and I moved to Santa Fe. Later, after I retired in 1996, I started re-reading it with greater interest. I believe the story is both enjoyable fiction and good history, and I hope you enjoyed it.

William C. Carson
Santa Fe, New Mexico
April 2002

Introduction to the 1965 Edition

Peter and Brownie Follow the Trace does not purport to be a factual history, but attempts merely to show some of the experiences and adventures that a boy of twelve might well have had if he had accompanied one of the wagon trains which crossed the Santa Fe Trail during the 1850s. In addition to my own observations, I have relied on the standard works dealing with the old Trail, especially *Down the Santa Fe Trail: The Diary of Susan Shelby Magoffin,* (edited by Stella M. Drumm); *Commerce of the Prairies,* Josiah Gregg; *Fort Union and the Winning of the Southwest,* Chris Emmett; and *Diary of My Journey from St. Louis to Santa Fe,* William Carr Lane (edited by Ralph E. Twitchell).

For valuable advice and assistance I am indebted to Mrs. Ernst A. Stadler, Archivist, Missouri Historical Society; Mrs. Alice Wallace, State Historical Society of Colorado; Mr. Homer F. Hastings, Superintendent, Fort Union National Monument; Mr. Joseph W. Snell, Curator of Manuscripts, Kansas State Historical Society; Mr. Rex L. Wilson, Archaeologist, Department of the Interior; Mr. Fred A. Voelker; and, above all, to my wife.

William G. B. Carson
St. Louis, Missouri
1965

Acknowledgments

Rather than putting the thanks to my family at the end of the acknowledgments, as seems to be common practice, I'm putting them first, particularly those to my wife, Georgia, and our daughters, Chapin and Laura. They have over many years had to endure detours during trips to "look at something," accompanied by a certain amount of grumpiness on my part.

In the background, of course, has always been my father, who had the original idea for the book and carried it through to completion. I'm sure that his determination to go to New Mexico and "look at things" resulted in our living here now.

Of more immediate assistance has been the interest and encouragement coming from Tom Chávez and Thomas Jaehn of the Palace of the Governors in Santa Fe, Anne Woodhouse of the Missouri Historical Society in St. Louis, Julian Suazo, Libby Stone, Dorothy Massey, Tony Lawson, Jim Idema, and Kay Carlson, all of whom have been enormously helpful by offering encouragement and advice.

William C. Carson
Santa Fe, New Mexico
April 2002

Biographical Sketches

As they made their way from St. Louis to Santa Fe and on towards Taos, the principal and fictional characters encountered various real and historic persons, some of whom played an important role in Peter's adventures.

Captain Isaac Bowen and his wife, **Kitty,** arrived at Fort Union in 1851, the year it was established. He was in charge of the Subsistence Department—she was the third woman at the Fort.

Major Robert Hall Chilton served in the United States Army from 1837 to 1861, when he resigned to fight for the Confederacy.

Bishop Juan Bautista Lamy arrived in Santa Fe in 1851. He became archbishop in 1875 and continued in the position for ten years. He died in 1888.

Wm. Carr Lane was named the second governor of the Territory of New Mexico on July 3, 1852, by President Millard Fillmore to succeed James. S. Calhoun, who had died the previous month while returning east over the Santa Fe Trail. Dr. Lane had already had a distinguished and adventurous career—pursuing Tecumseh and "The Prophet" with Colonel Russell in 1813, studying medicine at the University of Pennsylvania, and coming to Fort Bellefontaine near St. Louis with Morgan's Rifle Brigade. He then entered political life as the first mayor of St. Louis in 1823, was elected to seven more one-year terms, and served in the Missouri legislature. He was sixty-two when he came to New Mexico, bringing with him Frank Smith, whom he described as his "servant and friend." Miguel Antonio Otero served as the Governor's secretary. He was prominent in New Mexico affairs. His son of the same name was governor from 1897 to 1906. José Maria of the Pueblo of Tesuque also served him, often as an interpreter.

Solomon Jacob Spiegelberg was the eldest of the Spiegelberg brothers and first to come to Santa Fe, in 1844, to operate a mercantile establishment.

Señora Valdez had a hacienda in Embudo (now Dixon) in which Governor Lane was a guest during his travels about the territory.

Other real personages are mentioned to Peter at various points in the trip to help him understand the history of the country through which he was traveling.

William Bent, with his brother **Charles** and their partner Céran St. Vrain, had been trading with the Indians for many years when they established Bent's Old Fort in 1833. It was destroyed in 1849 after Charles's death. William Bent started building Bent's New Fort in 1853. He died in 1869.

Kit Carson served as a guide for General Frémont in 1842 and then served the Army as a guide and scout. He is controversial because of the campaign he led against the Navajos in 1863–64.

Chacon was chief of a band of Jicarilla Apaches camped near Abiquiu in 1853. They had started raiding in the surrounding area when the U.S. government failed to provide the provisions called for in an agreement.

Josiah Gregg traded on the Trail from 1831–1840 and was the author of Commerce on the Prairies.

General Stephen Watts Kearney led the American troops that conquered New Mexico in June 1846. He had already served in the army thirty-four years at that time. He was wounded later that year in California and died in St. Louis in 1848.

Samuel C. Owens formed a trading and mercantile partnership in 1846 with James Aull. He was killed during the Mexican War in 1847 at the Battle of Sacramento.

Colonel Edwin Vose Summer was the military commander in New Mexico when Governor Lane arrived. He refused to provide any support to the governor and maintained there was no civil government.

Peter encountered a number of Indian tribes during his journey—some friendly, some not so friendly. The cultures, ancestries, and histories of the tribes are long and complex. *The Encyclopedia of Native American Tribes*, Carl Waldman, Checkmark Books, 1999, is quite complete in describing them.

The **Apaches** were primarily nomadic hunters and gatherers roaming over much of the southwest. While their initial contacts with the Spanish were friendly, they developed into fierce warriors—the last band was not defeated by the U.S. Army until 1886.

The **Cheyenne** migrated gradually westward from Minnesota starting about 1700. They roamed more widely after gaining access to the horse. Many settled near Bent's Old Fort.

188

The **Comanches** ranged widely over the Great Plains after acquiring horses in the late 1600s and were greatly feared by both non-Indians and other tribes.

The **Navajo** occupied much of Northern Arizona and New Mexico and were greatly feared. Gradually, they changed to agricultural means of support, but continued raiding in the surrounding area. They were subdued in 1863 and removed to eastern New Mexico. Five years later they were allowed to return to their ancestral lands.

The **Pawnee** lived on the Great Plains, were friendly to the Americans, and often served as scouts against other tribes. They lived in villages part of the year, and roamed, hunting buffalo and raiding, at other times.

The **Pueblo Indians** lived in villages that were primarily agricultural and generally located along the Rio Grande River. Many exist today only as uninhabited ruins—such as Pecos—many others are active villages.

The **Sioux** came from four ancestral branches and lived on the Northern Plains. They have been noted in history because of their appearance, horsemanship, and two well-known battles with the United States Army—Little Bighorn and Wounded Knee. The Brulé were a band of one branch.

The **Utes** lived west of the Rocky Mountains. They were reputed to be fierce, but few Americans other than trappers encountered them until after 1845.

189

Selected Bibliography

It is probably impossible to know how many descriptions of the Santa Fe Trail and accounts of the hardships and adventures along the way have been published in the last 160 years—a bibliography compiled in 1971 included 718 entries—many more have appeared since.

The list below is not intended to be complete nor to include an example of all of the many and varied accounts. Rather, it is intended to identify some of the books considered in one sense to be classics and a few more recent publications to provide a starting point for anybody who wants to learn more about the country and history through which Peter traveled or as a guide to exploring certain aspects of the Trail as they now exist.

The books listed below were all originally published prior to 1966. Many have been re-published one or more times since they first appeared.

Commerce of the Prairies, Josiah Gregg, first appeared in 1844. It describes the journey, environment and people—some consider it the first great book of the West. It was most recently re-published by the University of Oklahoma Press.

The Old Trail to Santa Fe, Colonel Henry Inman, is another early, general account of the Trail. It first appeared in 1897 and is currently out of print.

Down the Santa Fe Trail and Into Mexico—The Diary of Susan Shelby Magoffin, edited by Stella M. Drumm, is an account of a young woman who started over the Trail with her husband in 1846. It first appeared in 1926 and is currently available through the University of Nebraska Press, 1982.

The Santa Fe Trail, R. L. Duffus, is another description of a Trail journey, first published in 1931 and now available from the University of New Mexico Press.

Bent's Fort, David Lavender, describes the two Bent's Forts and the trading and life at that point on the Trail. It first appeared in 1954 and is now available through University of Nebraska Press, 1972.

Matt Field on the Santa Fe Trail, collected by Clyde and Mae Reed Porter, edited by John E. Sunder, is a collection of journals and articles written by a young St. Louisan about his travels on the Trail in 1839. It first appeared in 1960 and is now available with a foreword by Mark L. Gardner through the University of Oklahoma Press, 1995.

Fort Union and the Winning of the Southwest, Chris Emmett, describes the history of the fort and its important role in the later years of the Trail. It first appeared in 1965 and is now out of print.

Two more recent books include much of the history of the Trail.

The Old Trail to Santa Fe, Marc Simmons, is a collection of essays concerning the Trail, University of New Mexico Press, 1996.

The Santa Fe Trail, David Dary, summarizes the history of the Trail from 1610 until the arrival of the railroads in the 1860s, Alfred A. Knopf, 2000.

There are innumerable maps and guides of all kinds that show the Trail in various levels of detail. Three that are particularly useful are:

Following the Santa Fe Trail, Marc Simmons and Hal Jackson, is a revised edition of a detailed guide that follows the Trail from Franklin, Missouri, to Santa Fe, with directions and sketches to help modern travelers find important sites, Ancient City Press, 2001.

Santa Fe Trail: Voyage of Discovery, Dan Murphy and Bruce Hucko, describes important points on the Trail and includes many current color photographs, K. C. Publications, 1998.

Santa Fe Trail, Official Map and Guide, National Park Service, provides an excellent map of the entire Trail in a pamphlet. Similar publications describe Park Service sites, e.g., Bent's Old Fort, Fort Union, Pecos.